Suddenly Cameron bent his head and whispered in her ear. 'Is it really you? I never thought I'd see you again.'

Meagan felt time stand still. She looked into his eyes and he grinned back at her. He raised an eyebrow, as if challenging her to admit she remembered him too. She knew without a shadow of doubt he was thinking about *that* night.

'I'm surprised you remember. It was a long time ago. And,' she couldn't help adding, 'that night obviously didn't mean much to you.'

He frowned again, and rested his hand on her shoulder. 'That's where you'd be wrong, Meagan,' he said softly. 'You are not a woman a man could easily forget.'

Anne Fraser was born in Scotland, but brought up in South Africa. After she left school she returned to the birthplace of her parents, the remote Western Islands of Scotland. She left there to train as a nurse, before going on to university to study English Literature. After the birth of her first child, she and her doctor husband travelled the world, working in rural Africa, Australia and Northern Canada. Anne still works in the Health Sector. To relax, she enjoys spending time with her family, reading, walking and travelling.

Recent titles by the same author:

HER VERY SPECIAL BOSS
DR CAMPBELL'S SECRET SON

POSH DOC
CLAIMS HIS BRIDE

BY
ANNE FRASER

MILLS & BOON®
Pure reading pleasure™

First published in Great Britain 2008
Large Print edition 2009
Harlequin Mills & Boon Limited,
Eton House, 18-24 Paradise Road,
Richmond, Surrey TW9 1SR

© Anne Fraser 2008

ISBN: 978 0 263 20524 4

Set in Times Roman 16½ on 19 pt.
17-0709-55086

Printed and bound in Great Britain
by CPI Antony Rowe, Chippenham, Wiltshire

POSH DOC
CLAIMS HIS BRIDE

CHAPTER ONE

As MEAGAN breathed in the heady aroma of peat smoke that drifted through her car window, she felt almost happy for the first time since Charlie had died. Maybe, just maybe, she could find some measure of peace and contentment on this remote Scottish island, which would be her home for the next few weeks and perhaps longer.

But, she thought as she glanced at her watch, she wasn't going to make a good first impression if she were late for her meeting with Dr MacDonald and his colleague. And she was going to be late unless the stream of cars that she had followed off the ferry went a bit faster than the ten miles an hour at which they were currently travelling. Incredibly, the cars in front slowed down even further—tourists unsure of the road, Meagan assessed exasperatedly.

Deciding to take action, she gunned her

powerful four-wheel-drive into second gear and, checking there was no oncoming traffic, began overtaking. It only took a fraction of second for her to realise her mistake—the cars had slowed down because the island road was reverting from two lanes to a single lane and there was no room to manoeuvre her Land Rover past the cars in front. Meagan did the only thing she could—she pumped her brakes and swung her vehicle hard to the left towards a lay-by. Everything would have still been OK had the recent rain not made the road greasy. Horrified, Meagan realised that she had lost traction and was heading for the ditch instead. At the last moment she closed her eyes, expecting the car to bounce or even flip, but— thank God—it was made of sterner stuff. Slowly it slid gently—almost gracefully—off the road and came to a rest with the nearside wheels on the tarmac and the offside wheels in the ditch, causing the car to tilt unnervingly to the side.

As the engine stalled, Meagan sat in stunned shock. She moved her limbs tentatively but luckily she didn't seem to have hurt herself. Before she had time to catch her breath, the pas- senger door was yanked open and a dark-haired man with concerned brown eyes leant in. Still shaking, she looked open-mouthed straight into the familiar set of eyes Cameron—the man who had occupied her thoughts for a long time after their first and only encounter all those years ago and whom she had never expected to see again, and certainly not within minutes of arriving on the island of Uist.

'Are you OK? Have you hurt yourself?' he asked, his voice cutting through her fog of confusion. *Perhaps I am concussed*, she thought, gingerly touching her forehead. *Maybe that's why I'm seeing Cameron in front of me. I'm concussed and mixing up the past with the present.*

Pinching the bridge of her nose and closing her eyes for a second, Meagan made herself breathe in deeply and slowly before opening her eyes again. *Keep calm, you're fine*, she told herself. As she looked once more into those gorgeous brown pools, she knew she hadn't been mistaken. It *was* Cameron. Apart from a narrowing of his eyes, he showed no sign that he recognised her. Could it be he had forgotten her? It *had* been several years and she knew she had changed. But surely not that much?

'Just sit still for a moment until we check you over,' Cameron said, reaching over the passenger seat to take a closer look.

'I'm fine. Thank you. A little shaken perhaps,' she replied, brushing his hands away. She was mortified to hear her voice tremble. 'Did anyone else go off the road?' she added anxiously, craning her neck to peer over his shoulder.

Reassured that she was unhurt, Cameron's initial concern was replaced with anger. 'No, but no thanks to you. What the bloody hell did you think you were doing, driving like a maniac on these roads? You could have killed yourself or worse still, someone else!'

His tone made Meagan's hackles rise. She knew she had been at fault, but who did he think he was to lecture her as if she were a child? She raised her chin and looked at him coolly. Could this angry, disdainful man really be the same one she had known before?

'Point taken. I'm fine. You can get on your way now. I'll manage,' she said, uncomfortably aware of how reckless she had been.

'Don't be a fool, woman.' Despite the words, Cameron's voice had softened. 'Come on, we'll help you get you back on the road. Hop out and we'll see what can be done.'

Meagan, still a little dazed, put up no further argument and stepped out, to her horror immediately sinking up to her ankles in the boggy peat that lined the road. She looked down at her feet in dismay. The new shoes she had bought in a fit of extravagance to celebrate her new job had all but disappeared beneath the sludge. She tried to pull them out, first one then the other, almost overbalancing in the process, but her feet refused to budge. She was trapped.

She thought that matters couldn't get any worse until she became aware that a crowd of onlookers had gathered as the occupants of the other cars left their vehicles to watch the proceedings. She lifted her eyes and found those of her rescuer, which, although moments before had looked at her sternly, were now twinkling with merriment, and although he tried to disguise it, a smile tugged at the corners of his generous mouth.

'Oh, go on, Cameron, help her out!' someone called out.

'Lend her your wellies, Cameron!' suggested another.

Meagan stood helplessly as Cameron, a broad grin lighting his face, stepped round to her side of the car, reached over and plucked her bodily from her muddy trap. As her feet came loose, she was imprisoned for a moment against his chest. He was so tall that despite her height of five feet eight she was still forced to look up into his eyes, even with her feet dangling above the ground. Held captive, Meagan could feel the heat of his body and the hardness of his muscles through the thin fabric of his sweater. It had been a long time since a man had held her in his arms. It had been even longer since this man had held her, but suddenly it felt like yesterday. To her dismay she felt a shock of desire that made her toes curl. Confused and mortified, she pushed against his chest with her hands.

Suddenly he bent his head and whispered in her ear, 'Is it really you? I never thought I'd see you again.'

Meagan felt time stand still. She looked into his eyes and he grinned back at her. He raised an eyebrow as if challenging her to admit she remembered him too. She knew without a shadow of doubt he was thinking about *that* night.

'Would you please put me down?' This was hardly the time or the place to reminisce about a night they had once shared. He was obviously enjoying making her look ridiculous. He held onto her for a second longer, looking into her eyes, amusement evident at her discomfort, before depositing her gently onto the road. As the audience clapped in appreciation of his gallantry, Meagan felt her cheeks burn with embarrassment. This was not how she had intended to introduce herself to the local population! These people were to be her patients and she cringed at the thought that she'd be the object of discussion and amusement around a lot of kitchen tables that evening. Cheeks blazing, she lifted her head high and tried to look like the professional career-woman she was. Cameron leapt into her Land Rover and with one great spray of mud—a good bit of which landed on Meagan— had all four wheels firmly back on the road. Thankfully, most of the crowd started to make their way back to their cars, satisfied that the drama was over.

Cameron left the engine running and walked back towards Meagan. Seeing her furiously trying to wipe some of the dirt off her suit, he laughed out loud.

'Good God—did I do that? I'm really sorry. Here, can I help?' He offered, taking a hankie from his jeans pocket. Gently tilting her chin with his fingertips, he wiped some of the mud from her face.

Meagan found herself yet again staring into his eyes, feeling even more foolish and totally off kilter. She could feel his breath on her face and the masculine scent of his strong, lean body as he stood close to her. Once again she felt a sharp tug of sheer unadulterated lust. Damn the man. Incredibly, after all these years he still had the ability to make her feel weak at the knees. Clearly the fright had awakened some dormant hormones she had been suppressing, she thought wryly. That was all. It was a well-known fact that adrenaline had that effect on people.

Desperate to regain her composure, she stepped back from Cameron, and managed a weak smile.

'Thanks for your help, I really appreciate it. I've really got to go now—I'm horribly late for my appointment as it is.' She was aware that she sounded as if she were at some afternoon tea party, but it was the best she could manage.

'No problem,' Cameron replied, his voice cooler this time, 'but, seriously, you have to take it easy on these narrow roads. I know that's a beast of a car you have, but brute strength in a vehicle is no substitute for a safe driver. Next time you—or some other unfortunate soul— might not be so lucky.'

Feeling like a five-year-old who had been caught stealing biscuits, and not a little indignant, Meagan climbed back into the driver's seat. She knew she had been at fault, but she was in no mood for a lecture from any man, no matter how helpful he had been, or how good-looking. And he was as gorgeous as she remembered, she couldn't help admitting to herself.

Liquid brown eyes and thick, black hair fell across his forehead, giving him an appealing air of vulnerability and sensuality that his solid frame belied. His broad shoulders were outlined in a V-neck black sweater that was thin enough for her to make out the contours of his muscular chest and a pair of faded blue jeans clung to his thighs in a most disconcerting manner. He had a stubble on his chin, as if he hadn't shaved for a few days. His thigh-high waders were turned down to below his knees and Meagan thought he looked like a fisherman—some sort of swash-buckling pirate in another life. But that wasn't what he had told her the night they had met.

Images came flooding back—the feel of his hands on her skin, the warmth of his body. She closed her eyes against the memory. It didn't matter how attractive he was, she was never going to get close to a man again—not after Charlie. Aware of the familiar ache that thinking of Charlie brought, she pushed him to the back of her mind. She was finished with men. In particular men who thought they were God's gift to women. And Cameron clearly belonged to that camp. That night had obviously meant nothing to him—he had never tried to get in touch with her afterward. Had there been many women? Had she just been one forgettable encounter of many? Meagan felt her cheeks burn at the thought. With an attempt at a nonchalant wave to her rescuer, she drove off more sedately. Confused and shaken, she refused to think about the night she had met Cameron and instead turned her thoughts to the meeting ahead.

Dr Colin MacDonald, or Dr Colin as she affectionately called him, and her father had been medical students together many years before and friends ever since. Dr Colin and his wife were going on an extended trip to Australia for four weeks, and when her father had told her that he was looking for a locum to help his partner while he was away, she had jumped at the chance. She had always wanted to return to Uist and hoped that some time on the peaceful and beautiful island on Scotland's west coast would help heal whatever it was that Charlie's death—and betrayal—seemed to have broken.

Dr Colin had suggested that they meet at the surgery for an informal interview at six that evening. 'It will just be Dr Stuart and myself, so it won't be formal. Perhaps we can grab a bite to eat afterwards,' he had suggested in his lilting Hebridean accent. 'As you know, I'll be leaving for Australia the next day, so unfortunately this will be the only chance the three of us will get to chat.'

Meagan pulled into the surgery car park. She glanced at her watch. With all that had happened she was most definitely late. She took a few minutes to collect herself while studying the surgery and its surroundings. It had changed from the old croft house that she remembered from her childhood visits. Instead, brand-new premises had been built more in keeping with modern-day practice. Nevertheless Meagan felt a pang of regret for the old practice with its homely feeling.

As she got out of the car, she glanced down at her feet. Around her ankles were matching rings of mud, like ankle-length boots. Her blouse and skirt were also spattered with brown. She'd have to sneak in, find the ladies and repair the damage before her interview. Late or not, there was no way she could present herself as an appropriate candidate for any job looking the way she did.

Quickly she fished around in her suitcase for a clean blouse, and digging out a pair of knee-length boots she swapped them for her high heels. At least they'd cover the worst of the damage. She crept into the surgery, blouse in hand, hoping to locate the ladies before bumping into anyone.

But it wasn't to be. Dr Colin MacDonald was waiting for her in the reception area.

'My dear girl,' he said, enveloping her in a

bear hug. 'I was getting worried about you. I checked with the ferry company and they told me the ferry had arrived right on time. Was the traffic on the way here awful?'

Thankfully he didn't seem to require a reply. Meagan wasn't sure she wanted him to know she had managed to go off the road so soon after her arrival.

'I'm here now—that's what matters,' she said, returning his hug. 'It's so good to see you, Dr Colin—and to be back on Uist again.'

'Here,' he said, holding her by the arms. 'Let me get a good look at you—Dr Galbraith now, no less. The last time I saw you was at your wedding, when you were still slogging away as a junior doctor.'

Meagan must have looked stricken, as his voice immediately softened. Gathering her gently back into his arms, he soothed her, 'My dear girl, I'm so sorry. Your father told me all about Charlie.'

Meagan breathed in deeply, gently disengaging herself from his embrace.

'I'm all right now, Dr Colin, really. It just hits me now and again. But I'm here and ready to start afresh! Or at least I will be in a few moments,' she said, remembering the state of her clothes. She looked around anxiously, but there was no one else in sight. Perhaps Dr Stuart was waiting in one of the consulting rooms to start the meeting?

'Dr Colin, if you don't mind, could I nip into the ladies quickly? I don't want to keep you and Dr Stuart waiting, but I need to freshen up.'

Luckily Colin wasn't the sort of man to pay much attention to a woman's appearance. Meagan remembered his long-suffering wife Peggy complaining often that Colin would see patients in his slippers if it weren't for her. And, right enough, Meagan couldn't help noticing that his sweater was a bit worse for wear around the elbows. Nevertheless, Meagan knew Colin gave his patients his undivided attention and was loved in return.

'You take your time, my dear,' he said. 'Dr Stuart's been held up on his way back from a weekend's fishing. He phoned me on the surgery phone just now—I can't be doing with these portable things. Anyway, he'll be here as soon as he can, but there's plenty of time for you to sort yourself out and for me to show you our new premises, so don't rush.'

In the sanctuary of the ladies, Meagan repaired the damage as best she could. It was unfortunate, but not the end of the world, that she had been seen not looking her best. She grimaced at her reflection in the mirror. She had to admit she had neglected her appearance for a long time after Charlie's death and besides working abroad, where there often hadn't been even basic facilities to wash, it would have been impossible to be perfectly turned out, even if she'd cared to.

But determined that this would be a new start she had treated herself to a new wardrobe, a very expensive haircut and an extortionate but heavenly weekend at a spa. She was pleased with the feathery haircut that framed her face, emphasising her best feature—her green eyes. It deflected attention away from her too-wide mouth, she thought with satisfaction. Pity about the new shoes, however. They were ruined.

Not wanting to keep Colin waiting any longer than she had already, she sprayed perfume behind her ears and went to join him.

'Dr Stuart's just arrived. He's waiting for us in

our seminar room. Perhaps he can give you the guided tour tomorrow instead. We'll have a quick chat, then you're coming to dinner—Peggy's expecting you. Afterwards, I'll show you the way to the cottage I've rented for you. Is that all right?'

Colin had already gone over the arrangements with Meagan on the phone as he and Peggy were leaving the next day on the first leg of their trip, which would take in Australia as well as visits to their daughters in Glasgow and London on the way. Meagan knew they had both been looking forward to it for some time. They had had some difficulty attracting a locum, and when he had heard from Meagan's father that she was looking for a short-term position with a view to a permanent post, he'd been determined to entice her to the island.

Colin ushered Meagan into the meeting room, standing aside for her to go in first. As Meagan entered the first thing that caught her attention was the man sitting at one end of the table. He may have showered and shaved—that much was evident from the longish black hair clinging damply to his forehead—and he may now be wearing a crisp white shirt and she noticed as he stood to greet her, freshly laundered beige chinos, but there was no mistaking him. It was Cameron! For a moment Meagan let her jaw drop. It was all she could do to stop herself groaning out loud. Cameron, the man who had stolen her heart all those years ago, Cameron, the man who had rescued her by the roadside, was Dr Stuart—her new colleague. Meagan felt her heart pound as she wondered frantically how to handle this new development. While her mind whirled about whether she should acknowledge to Dr Colin that the two of them had already met, Cameron's deep tone broke the lengthening silence.

'Dr Galbraith, I presume,' he said, a half-smile on his lips. 'I trust you had a pleasant journey? I'm sorry I was late but there was a hold-up on the road. Some visitor to the island managed to put her car in the ditch and she needed some help.' Out of sight of Colin, he dropped his lid in a slow wink.

Speechless, Meagan could only allow him to engulf her hand in his and shake it. So this is how he wanted to play it, she thought with relief.

'Please, sit down. I don't think this will take

too long. As you know, Colin is leaving tomorrow. Circumstances prevented us from meeting before now, but he has assured me you are right for the job. He said you are practical, sensible, as well as an excellent doctor. All welcome traits in a colleague,' he said dryly. Meagan couldn't be sure, but thought he was mocking her.

She sat down on the nearest chair, wishing she had some time to gather her thoughts. Oblivious of the tension between his the younger doctors, Colin addressed Cameron.

'You know, Cameron, we are fortunate to get Meagan. Her father has been trying to persuade her to join him in his private practice in Edinburgh but without success so far, eh, Meagan?'

'I hate to disappoint my father, but city life just isn't for me,' Meagan said. 'And after the time I've just spent abroad I'm more sure than ever that I want to work somewhere where I can really do some good and be part of the community as well.'

'I notice you're wearing a wedding ring. Is your husband joining you in Uist while you're here?' Cameron asked suddenly.

The question took Meagan completely by surprise, although she supposed it was perfectly reasonable of him to ask.

She darted a glance at Colin. He obviously hadn't mentioned her past to Cameron.

Meagan swallowed. She still wasn't used to saying the words 'I'm a widow' and she didn't want to go into any explanations now. Instead, she evaded his probing, but nevertheless her answer was truthful. 'No, he won't be joining me.'

Cameron frowned slightly. He looked as if he was about to say something, but then changed the subject.

'I'm concerned you may find us a little boring here. I gather from Colin that you trained in London and have just returned after a two-year stint with Médecins Sans frontiéres?' Cameron said quietly. 'I spent some time with them myself and you couldn't have more of a contrast here. Although—' he glanced at Colin '—we do have our moments.'

Meagan looked at him a stubborn set to her chin. 'I'm quite sure I won't be bored. In many ways this will be the perfect opportunity to see if rural life suits me before I decide where to join a permanent practice.' She managed a smile while forcing herself to look steadily into those deep brown eyes. 'Besides, I'm a keen sailor,' she went on, 'and I'm never happier then when I'm near the sea. I always hoped to return to Uist one day. I just never dreamt it would be as one of the medical team.' Meagan couldn't help sliding a look in Cameron's direction. When she had met him she had been with a group of fellow sailors towing the islands. He had known that. Still there wasn't a flicker in his eyes.

'Colin did mention that you had been here before, so at least you know what to expect.'

'Meagan sailed competitively, Cameron. She's a woman of many talents.' Colin smiled fondly at Meagan. 'I still have my old boat if ever you want to use it. I don't get out in it much these days,' he said, rubbing his hip with a grimace, 'but Cameron takes care of her for me. I'm sure he'd be delighted to take you out on it. Won't you, Cameron?'

Cameron smiled, his eyes creasing at the corners. 'It would be my pleasure, but I suspect we'll both be too busy while you're away to do much sailing. Anyway, shall we get down to business?'

The next hour passed swiftly as Cameron quizzed Meagan on her experience. She knew that there was little he could find to criticise, except perhaps her limited experience as a general practitioner. She hadn't actually worked as a GP since she'd completed her general practice training. The end of her training had coincided with Charlie's death, and once she had emerged from her haze of grief she had gone overseas. While her experience there had shown her she could cope with most things, working as a GP was bound to have its own challenges.

Colin leaned back in his chair, apparently satisfied that the interview was drawing to a close.

'The practice covers the whole of Uist, with a population of around two thousand, a large proportion of whom is elderly. We can handle most things but what we can't handle comfortably we send to Stornoway, or for more specialist care to Glasgow. We're very fortunate to have Cameron, who is a member of the Royal College of Paediatricians and who is happy to see most of the children,' Colin informed Meagan.

Meagan looked over at Cameron in surprise. What was a qualified paediatrician doing in rural practice? she wondered. But something in his expression warned her not to pursue the matter.

'We do our own on-call rota and I'm afraid that's one in two at the moment,' Colin went on 'You'll have every second night and weekend on and every second one off. Do you feel you can cope?'

'That's fine. I'm used to working hard. I prefer to keep busy,' Meagan said. It was the truth. Working so hard that she had no time for thinking had been what had saved her sanity.

Colin looked satisfied. 'Well, that's sorted, then. Take tomorrow to settle in and then make a start the day after. Now let's go and get some dinner, shall we? I'm sure you're ready for it, Meagan, after your long journey. Peggy is looking forward to seeing you. Are you sure you won't join us, Cameron? You know they'll be plenty.'

'No, thanks, Colin. I need to get home. But give my love to Peggy and both of you have a wonderful holiday. Don't worry about us here. We'll be fine. I'll look in on you tomorrow at some point, Meagan. Perhaps show you around, if you like?' Cameron said. He stood, stretching his lean frame.

'I'll look forward to it,' Meagan said politely.

'Goodnight, then,' he said leaving Meagan and Colin alone.

Meagan watched his departing back, before turning back to Colin.

'Are you sure he wants me here?' she said anxiously.

'He wasn't altogether keen,' Colin admitted reluctantly. 'Nothing personal, you understand. He just thought we should have asked someone a little more…well, settled. He knows I am looking to retire and that we need a replacement for me. He's worried that a young single woman won't stay and he's also little worried you don't have enough experience for the job.'

Meagan's heart sank. Her day was going from bad to worse. On top of everything, it seemed that Cameron had opposed her appointment. Had it simply been her lack of experience or had he known who she was? He had shown no indication that he'd known she was the new locum when they had met on the road, and there was no reason for him to associate her married name, Dr Galbraith, with Meagan Davidson. And what about him? Was he married? She swallowed a sigh. If she had known that she would find Cameron here, would she still have come? She had taken the job because she had thought it would be a fresh start, and the last thing she needed were complications. And somehow she recognised with a shiver that working with Cameron was going to be a complication she could do without. Still, it was too late now. She was here. At least until Colin returned from his trip.

Colin must have noticed how dejected she felt because he added hastily, 'I'm sure once he gets to know you he'll recognise that you are the right person for the job and then you'll get on famously. You have a lot in common. Until then, try not to worry. Cameron will see you come to no harm. You can trust him with your life.'

But, as Meagan followed Colin out of the surgery, she wasn't altogether sure she could trust herself.

As Cameron drove home he was thinking about his new colleague. It had been a surprise when he had recognised the woman in the car. And an even bigger shock to find that she was the new locum. He had known her as Meagan Davidson, now she was Meagan Galbraith. She had married, then, but where was her husband? Were they separated? Divorced? Why had she come alone?

Even before he'd realised who the locum was, he'd had grave reservations about taking on someone with her level of experience. And it wasn't just her relative lack of general practice experience that had worried him. She was clearly used to a more exciting life than the one she'd find here. Why had she come? And how did he feel about seeing her again?

Despite the lines of pain etched into the corners of her mouth—and he wondered what had caused them—she looked even younger than her 26 years. She had no idea of how vulnerable she appeared, especially, he thought amused, with the small smear of dirt on her brow that had escaped her cleaning efforts. Notwithstanding the odd blob of dirt, she looked more like a fashion icon from the city than a country doctor.

A practice like theirs couldn't afford passengers. He had wanted to recruit someone older, more experienced, but there hadn't been many applicants. Cameron had been carrying an increased share of the practice burden for the last year as Colin had relinquished more and more to his younger partner.

Cameron had known about Colin's friendship with the new locum's father and had been concerned that the friendship might have influenced the older doctor's decision, but Colin had been adamant that Meagan was an exceptional junior doctor who had passed all her exams with distinction. So, despite his reservations, he had agreed to go along with his partner's choice. And that choice had turned out to be more interesting than he could ever have suspected. Well, it was done now. He would just have to keep a close eye on Meagan and be there to offer support to her and the patients whenever possible. And as for the fact she still made his pulse race? That was just male libido, he told himself firmly, and the fact he had been too long without a woman. It was nothing whatsoever to do with eyes the colour of the sea after rain and a mouth made for kissing. Nothing whatsoever.

CHAPTER TWO

IT TOOK Meagan a couple of seconds to realise where she was when she woke up the next morning. It had been dark when Colin had dropped her off the night before and, exhausted, she had gone straight to bed. Despite her tiredness, she had lain awake, thinking about Cameron. Why had he never tried to get in touch with her? She had been so sure that he had felt the same way she had that night they had met. She had waited for him to contact her, but eventually anticipation had turned into disappointment with the realisation he was never going to. She had been badly mistaken about him and the kind of man he was. Now he was here and they'd be working together and, God, help her, he still made her feel week at the knees.

The day stretched before her to do as she pleased. Determined to make the most of it, she jumped out of bed and headed for the shower. Once she was dressed she would spend the day re-exploring the island and refamiliarising herself with her surroundings.

The cottage Colin had arranged for her was a renovated black house. Although it was tiny—with a small bedroom on one side and a kitchen/living room on the other and a bathroom in the middle—it was very cosy. There was just about enough room for her and her suitcases—if she was very organised. The sitting room had an open fire that Meagan surveyed with some trepidation. She hadn't a clue how to go about setting and lighting a fire. Next to the fire, which had been set ready to light, was a basket of peat and some kindling. The same person had also left a basket of provisions, including, Meagan noted, coffee, milk, scones and even pancakes for her breakfast.

Meagan dressed warmly after her quick shower, surveying her appearance in the long mirror in the corner of her bedroom. She had pulled on her old but still stylish jeans, which she knew emphasised her long legs and slim figure. She straightened her hair until it fell to her shoulders in a sleek curtain and darkened her lashes with black mascara. That was all the make-up she normally wore, unless she was going out somewhere in the evening when she would add glossy red lipstick. To complete her outfit for walking the moors, she grabbed her green jacket in case the weather changed to rain, and pulled on her favourite leather boots.

Stepping out the front door, she gasped with surprise and pleasure. It had been dark when she had arrived the night before and she hadn't been aware of how her new home was situated. She was delighted to see that the house had been built on a piece of land that projected into the sea, giving the impression that it was on its own small island. The day was glorious. Bright sunlight reflected on the water, which hugged the shore on three sides, turning it from deep blue to aquamarine where the waves lapped the shore. She listened to the sensuous sound of the waves gently washing over the rocks and a the feeling of peace wash over her.

The back of the house was sheltered from the wind by some rowan trees and had the best view. Meagan could imagine spending her evenings sitting outside, watching the wildlife as the sun went down. At the front was a rough drive leading up to the main road. A few sheep grazed, lazily turning disinterested eyes on Meagan before returning their attention to the grass. The place was perfect. Perhaps here she could at last really begin to put the past behind her.

Hearing a car's engine, Meagan looked around and watched a battered Land Rover making its way down the track to the house. The car pulled up and a tall, elegant woman wearing faded jeans and wellingtons got out.

The woman eyed Meagan for a moment before extending a hand.

'Hi, you must be Dr Galbraith,' she said. 'I'm Rachel—from Grimsay House.' She indicated an imposing building on the top of the hill with a nod of her head.

She was one of the most beautiful women Meagan had ever seen. Long blonde hair hung to her shoulders, framing high cheekbones and sculpted lips. Violet eyes were accentuated with thick dark lashes that looked as if they owed nothing to mascara. Beside her, Meagan felt plain if not downright dowdy.

'Pleased to meet you.' Meagan took the proffered hand, aware of the briefest pressure before her hand was relinquished.

'I'm sorry to impose on your day off but Jessie—the cook—her daughter's not feeling well and she wanted Cameron to have a look at her. Unfortunately he's tied up with another patient. He asked us to ring you instead, but I thought I may as well pop down in person and give you a lift. If you're free, that is?' Cool eyes regarded Meagan steadily. Meagan surmised that this was a woman who expected people to do as she asked.

'I'd be happy to see her. If you could give me a moment, I'll get my bag.'

Uninvited, Rachel followed her inside the house.

'Its years since I was in here,' she said. 'I'd forgotten how tiny it is. It used to be a staff cottage.'

'I think its lovely,' Meagan said, collecting her bag from the sitting room. 'Absolutely perfect.' Inexplicably Meagan felt defensive about her new home. 'Shall we go?'

The journey took just a few minutes. There was only enough time for Rachel to point a few landmarks out to Meagan before they were at their destination.

As Rachel swung the Land Rover into the large gravel car park of Grimsay House, Meagan marvelled at the majestic building before her. To describe it as a house was rather like referring to Mount Vesuvius as a steaming kettle. Two elegant stone columns framed wide stone steps leading up to a beautiful oak door at the entrance. Honey-coloured stonework hinted at the imposing age of the building. Meagan noted gentle puffs of smoke emanating from the large gable chimneys at either end of the house, which was framed by a breath-taking tangle of trees, shrubs and wildflowers. Dragging her eyes away, Meagan gathered up her medical bag as she followed Rachel inside the house and into the flag-stoned entrance hall.

'It's beautiful,' Meagan said, taking in the elegant furniture and ornate framed portraits that graced the walls.

'I suppose,' Rachel said dismissively. 'Can't say I notice it much any more. Jessie and Effie are up here.'

Meagan followed Rachel up two flights of stairs into a bedroom that led off a narrow hall. The bedroom was light and airy and pleasantly furnished. On the large bed covered with a pink quilt on which elephants and rabbits gambolled, lay a small, pale child of around seven. Sitting next to the child, holding a book, sat a woman in her twenties who Meagan took to be Effie's mother.

'This is Jessie and her daughter Effie. Jessie, Effie—Dr Galbraith,' Rachel made the introductions. She then strode towards the window and looked out, turning her back on the proceedings.

Jessie stood up. 'Thank goodness you're here,' Jessie said. 'Effie's been complaining of stomach ache since the early hours of this morning. I've given her paracetamol but it hasn't helped. Now she's being sick.' Jessie spoke quickly, clearly anxious. She turned to her daughter, who was watching Meagan with solemn eyes. 'Effie, Dr Galbraith is here to see if we can make you better,' Jessie continued.

Meagan approached the bed and smiled warmly at the young girl. Crouching next to her, she reached over to stroke the large pink cuddly toy the child was clutching.

'A girl after my own heart, I see,' she said soothingly. 'You know, I had a bunny rabbit just like that when I was your age.'

Effie peeked out at Meagan from behind the rabbit. 'My tummy hurts,' she said plaintively, 'and I've been sick. Four times,' she added proudly.

'Well, we'll have to see what we can do about that. If you lie down flat, I'd like to feel your tummy.'

Uncertainly, Effie looked towards Jessie.

'Go on, *mo ghaol*,' Jessie encouraged.

The child responded, sliding down in bed and pulling up her pyjama top for Meagan.

Meagan examined her, gently feeling for any abdominal tenderness and looking down the child's throat for signs of inflammation. She was unable to find any abnormality and when she checked the child's pulse and temperature she was pleased to find both normal.

'OK, Effie, that's you. I don't think there is anything to worry about, but I'm going to ask your mummy to keep you in bed for the rest of the day and maybe tomorrow. Don't try and eat anything but take small sips of water whenever you can manage it and I'll pop back tomorrow to see how you are.'

Turning towards Jessie, Meagan signalled to her to step outside with her.

'I'm sure it's nothing to worry about—probably a bug that's going around. I'll leave you my telephone numbers. Please, don't hesitate to call if there's any change in Effie's condition. But I suspect in a day or two she'll be as right as rain.'

Jessie sighed with relief. 'Oh, thank goodness. I know it's silly to worry, but she's all I've got.'

'Just keep her in bed and let her sleep,' Meagan said. 'I'll be surprised if she's not back to her usual self by tomorrow.'

As Meagan turned to go, Jessie said, 'Do you have time for a cup of tea? I know I could do with one! I'll just check with Rachel that she's happy to sit with Effie for a bit,' she said, popping her head back round the door.

Apparently reassured that her presence wasn't needed, she led Meagan back downstairs.

'Don't worry about tea,' Meagan said. 'I'm sure you have plenty to be getting on with.'

'I could do with a cup. I've been up most of the night.' She yawned. 'Really, you'd be doing me a favour. A chat would stop me conking out. I've still got Sunday lunch to prepare.'

Following Jessie into the kitchen at the back

of the house, Meagan took a seat at the large oak table that dominated the centre of the room. Black and white tiles patterned the floor and at centre stage stood a double-oven Aga. Meagan waited silently as Jessie bustled about the kitchen, spooning tea into a pot and setting cups out onto a tray. Now that anxiety no longer furrowed her face, Meagan could see that she was very pretty, her curly auburn hair framing a delicate face with large, gentle green eyes.

'The house is gorgeous. I gather from Rachel you are the cook here.'

Jessie nodded, placing a china cup in front of Meagan and pushing the sugar bowl and milk jug towards her. 'Effie and I love it. It's been in the family for generations—and it's hardly a house, more like a manor really. But the late laird never liked anyone to refer to it as such. He didn't want the locals to think he thought himself or anyone else in his family above them. Unfortunately, when he died inheritance tax took a fair chunk of the family fortune, and it's been a bit of a struggle for them to keep the estate running. But it's a labour of love for Cameron and Simon, rather than a millstone around their necks.' Her tone softened. 'Their mother died years ago, when the children were very young, poor souls. So apart from them, there's myself and Mrs McLeod, the housekeeper—she looks after your cottage too. The rest of the staff come in on a daily basis.'

Meagan was confused. What did Cameron have to do with Grimsay House?

Jessie continued chatting while she poured the tea and buttered some scones. 'Grimsay House is open to visitors during the summer. It helps make ends meet and we have shooting and fishing parties coming to stay too. We also put on the odd ceilidh in the grand hall as well as an end-of-summer ball, which is actually at the end of the month. All in all it keeps me pretty busy.'

'Er, Jessie. You mentioned Cameron. Surely you don't mean Dr Stuart?'

Jessie looked at Meagan keenly. 'You mean you don't know?' She must have seen Meagan's look of confusion. 'Cameron—Dr Stuart— being the eldest son, inherited the estate from his father. Our own Dr Stuart is actually Lord Grimsay of Grimsay house.' Seeing the look of shock on Meagan's face, she gave a low whistle.

'You really didn't know, did you? Well, I guess there is no reason why you should. Cameron keeps the two sides of his life pretty separate. He always wanted to be a doctor. Ever since he was a small boy. But since his father died, he has taken on the responsibilities he inherited. Somehow he manages the two roles.'

Meagan almost choked on her tea. Cameron. A lord! As if it hadn't been a big enough shock finding out he was her colleague—now this. He hadn't said anything about it that night, so on top of everything he hadn't even been honest with her. Was that why he had never contacted her? What would a lord want with a student, a nobody? Hardly a long-term prospect for someone in his position. She hadn't even been here twenty-four hours and the shocks kept coming.

Meagan's mind whirled. 'No, I didn't know.' She paused, even more confused. And where did the beautiful Rachel fit in to all of this? Aware that Jessie was looking at her with anticipation, she dragged her mind back to the conversation. 'But isn't it unusual for someone in his position to have a career?'

'Not really. Not up here. The family has always lived as part of the community. Every so often they go to London, and of course they have friends up. But if you knew Cameron, you'd know he isn't the kind of man to want an idle life. He has to be doing something. Something that really matters.'

Jessie passed Meagan a scone. Meagan bit into one, realising as she did so that she hadn't had breakfast before Rachel had appeared and was suddenly ravenous. Munching the scone gave her a little time to absorb what Jessie had just told her.

'These are delicious, Jessie,' she said. 'Someone left some pancakes for me at the cottage—were they yours?'

'Yes. Mrs Macleod and I thought you might like some to welcome you. I bake a batch at least once a day. Apart from the visitors, there is always someone prowling around the kitchen. She stopped, cocking an ear. 'Speaking of which, that sounds like Cameron.'

Meagan looked around, surprised. Sure enough, Jessie was right. Cameron came into the kitchen, sniffing the air appreciatively. 'Ha, in the nick of time.' He reached for one of the scones.

Jessie batted his hand away with a playful tap. 'No, you don't. I've only just made enough for this afternoon. I only gave Dr Galbraith one seeing as she was kind enough to give up her free morning to come and see Effie.'

'And how is Effie?' Cameron asked. He waited until Jessie had turned to fill the kettle again before filching a scone.

'She's fine,' Meagan answered. 'Just an upset tummy. I've recommended a day in bed. I expect she'll be fine by tomorrow.'

'Rachel's keeping her company while I look after Dr Galbraith. I'll take over in a minute.'

Meagan noticed Cameron's raised brow at the mention of Rachel's name.

'It was either that or she'd have to finish the baking.' Jessie and Cameron shared a smile.

'Rachel baking? Never in a month of Sundays.' He swallowed the last of his scone. 'I'll pop in and see Effie, shall I?' Cameron suggested.

'Oh, don't worry. If Dr Galbraith thinks she's OK then that's all right by me. If you go up, she'll start to think there's something really wrong.'

'In that case, why don't I show Meagan around?'

Meagan started. 'Oh, please. Don't put yourself to any trouble. I'm sure you have enough to do. I can look around on my own another time—if that's all right?' She didn't know why, but she was loath to be alone with Cameron. She suddenly felt awkward in his presence.

Cameron ignored Meagan's protest and glanced down at her feet with the air of an expert.

'Those boots are no use for walking here. There's a pair of wellingtons in the hall. They belong to Rachel. You look as if you have roughly the same size feet. I'm sure she'll be happy for you to borrow them.'

Meagan wasn't sure that Rachel was the kind of woman who was happy to share anything with another woman, even a pair of wellington boots, but as Cameron took hold of her elbow and gently but firmly propelled her out of the kitchen, she decided for the moment at least it was better to take the line of least resistance. There would be time later to show Cameron Stuart she wasn't a woman who took kindly to being bossed around.

The air smelled of the sea and the sun felt warm on her face as they made their way from the back of the house and headed up the hill. She had tried on Rachel's wellington boots, but they had proved much too small. Cameron had forced her to try on a pair of his, but just like Goldilocks she had found them much too big. Just when Meagan had thought with a sigh of relief that the walk would have to be abandoned, Cameron had triumphantly produced a pair belonging to one of the farm workers that, while a little large, would do. As Meagan clomped along beside Cameron, she struggled to keep up with his long strides.

She felt the silence between them was awkward. Should she bring up that night they had shared all those years ago? But what would she—could she—say? Perhaps he didn't want to be reminded of it. Instead, she decided to stay on safer ground.

'Jessie was telling me a little bit about the house and how it's been in the family for generations. I had no idea who you were.'

Cameron narrowed his eyes as her. 'Does it make a difference? As far as you and the locals are concerned, I'm Dr Stuart, or just Cameron. My other life—this—' he indicated the land with a sweep of his hand '—has nothing to do with my medical life. I think of myself as lucky. To be able to do the job I love in a place I love.'

As they reached the top of the hill, Cameron turned to her and said, 'Enough about me. What about you? I always wondered if you'd succeeded in becoming a doctor, although I was pretty sure that you wouldn't let anything stand in your way. You appeared to be a woman who knew exactly what she wanted.' He turned the full gaze of his interested brown eyes on her and gave her an appraising look. 'I have to say it was a bit of a surprise to find you on the side of the road.' He grinned then frowned. 'And an even bigger shock to find out we'd be working together.'

Meagan was relieved that he had brought it up. It saved her from having to decide if, and how, to raise the topic. However, his words were a reminder of how little importance he had placed on their first meeting.

'You hid it well, then,' Meagan retorted. 'Anyway, I'm surprised you remember. It was a long time ago. And,' she couldn't help adding, 'that night obviously didn't mean much to you.'

He frowned again and rested his hand on her

shoulder. 'That's where you'd be wrong, Meagan,' he said softly. 'You are not a woman a man could easily forget.'

But why did you never contact to me? Meagan wanted to ask. If it meant anything at all? But pride stilled the words. He hadn't contacted her. She had meant nothing to him. She would never let him see how much it had hurt her.

Cameron watched as the emotions chased across Meagan's face. He had hurt her, he knew that. She was as beautiful as he remembered but there was sadness and a reticence that hadn't been there in the younger, passionate Meagan. Life had changed her. He didn't know how or why, but he knew, in time, he would find out. This woman still had the ability to make his pulse race as no other woman had before or since. And there had been many women. Heaven knew, he was no saint but he had felt all those years before and still felt that there was something different about this woman.

'I know what I said back then. And I meant it,' Cameron said softly. 'I was going to contact you. But then…well, I guess you could say life got in the way.' He looked into the distance, his eyes bleak. Then it was as if a shutter came down. Almost absent-mindedly he reached for her arm, stroking the soft flesh of her inner arm with his roughened thumb. 'I never thought I would see you again. Tell me about yourself. You're married now.' He paused, almost as if he didn't want to ask the next question. 'Are you happy?' he asked softly.

At his touch Meagan felt a shiver of desire go through her—there was still something about this man that set her nerve endings on fire. He made her feel wanted and attractive again. As if the shock of Charlie's death in a car accident hadn't been enough, finding out that he had been killed with his mistress beside him had almost destroyed her. She had known that their marriage had not been happy for some time, but she had never suspected that he was being unfaithful to her. The knowledge had made her lose confidence, not just in her ability to trust people but in herself and her own femininity. Now, for the first time in the two years since Charlie had died, she was aware of herself once more as a desirable woman. Meagan had to admit to herself that it felt good—but it was all wrong. She didn't want to feel anything for another man ever again. Least of all this one. She seemed destined to fall for the wrong men. Well, she was older and wiser now. She knew better than to give her heart to any man.

In her confusion, Meagan jerked away from him and, catching her foot on a rock, stumbled. Cameron caught her just before she fell and pulled her against him. She could smell the faint tang of his aftershave and feel the rough wool of his sweater against her cheek. For a moment she let herself rest against him, feeling safe for the first time in two years.

'What is it?' he asked, tipping her chin up with one finger so he could see more clearly into her eyes.

The kindness of his voice along with the memories of Charlie caused her eyes to fill and he traced the track of a tear down her cheek with his thumb.

Pulling away, Meagan blinked away the tears. 'I was married—but he died. In a car accident.'

'Oh, Meagan. I am so sorry,' Cameron said. 'Colin didn't tell me very much about the new locum. All he told me was that you were the daughter of a close friend. He never said much more and I never asked.'

'I asked him not to say anything. I've had enough of people's pity. Part of the attraction about coming here was that people wouldn't know anything about me. I wanted it to be a new start…' She tailed off.

'Hey, hey,' he said softly. 'It's OK. I won't tell anyone. We doctors are used to keeping other people's secrets. Although—' he shook his head and smiled ruefully '—you'll find out soon enough it's almost impossible to keep a secret on this island. The locals have a habit of finding things out. And as for us…um…meeting before, I think that's also best kept in the past and between us, don't you?'

As Meagan looked into his eyes her thoughts flashed back to their 'meeting', as he had put it.

She remembered every detail. She had wondered for years about the man she had known simply as Cameron. Then she had met Charlie and buried her memories. Now, with Cameron here in front of her once more, she let the memories come flooding back.

She had been in her final year of medicine,

spending her last free summer sailing around the Western Isles. It had been the last night of the crew's stay on Uist before they were due to sail home. By chance they had discovered that there was to be a beach barbeque at Coola Bay—a fabulous stretch of golden, sandy beach on the north side of the island.

By the time they arrived at the barbeque, the sun was beginning to sink, turning the sky pink and purple. A large crowd had already assembled and several groups stood around fires, laughing and chatting. Meagan sniffed the air appreciatively as the smell of sizzling sausages and chicken scented the sea air.

Meagan left her circle of friends, wanting to savour her last sunset on the island. As the sun melted into the sea, her attention was drawn to a young man who stood in a group of lively partygoers. It wasn't simply that he was tall, topping everyone else by a good couple of inches, or good-looking—although he was both—there was something in his manner that made him stand out from the crowd. He seemed to radiate confidence and self-assurance.

Meagan watched him surreptitiously from

beneath her lashes. He had thick black hair worn slightly too long so that it flopped over one eye. As he laughed and joked with his friends Meagan could see dimples in both cheeks which appeared, disappeared and reappeared again.

He must have become aware of her staring because all at once he turned his gaze on her and slowly let his left eyelid droop in a wink. She had never seen anything quite as sexy and was mortified to feel her cheeks go pink. Clearly amused by her discomfort, his smile broadened into a grin, emphasising his dimples. After holding her gaze for a moment, he let his eyes travel slowly over her slim body, resting on her breasts before continuing down her shapely legs and back up to her eyes. Despite her annoyance at his blatant evaluation, Meagan felt herself unable to move under his scrutiny. Then with a quip to his friends that made them laugh, he began to make his way over to her with long easy strides.

Hot with confusion, Meagan turned on her heel, seeking the relative safety of her friends, but before she had taken more than a couple of steps she felt a strong grip on her upper arm.

'Not thinking of leaving, are you?' murmured a soft, deep voice in her ear. Taking a gulp of air to steady her breathing, Meagan turned towards him, but to her consternation found herself so close she could smell the soap on his skin and the sea in his hair.

'Don't go' was all he said.

The rest of the evening passed in a blur for Meagan. Cameron didn't leave her side, giving her his undivided attention and flirting outrageously, demanding that she dance only with him to the swirling tunes that were played by guests who had brought instruments with them.

Eventually the tempo of the music slowed and he pulled Meagan close, wrapping her arms around his neck and nuzzling hers in return as he trickled his fingers along her back. Powerless to resist, Meagan let her body melt into his and raised her face, staring into his eyes, which reflected the flickering light of the bonfires around them.

With a muttered cry of something in Gaelic, he bent his head to hers and claimed her lips with kisses that were gentle at first but, as she responded, grew increasingly demanding.

She could feel his body grow hard with his desire and her own body responded as if she had no control over it as she clung to him, seeking more and more of him until finally, with a groan, he pulled away from her and, taking her by the hand, said softly, 'Come with me.'

There was something about him that made Meagan feel less than her nineteen years. It wasn't just that he was older—four or five years older than her, she guessed. Perhaps it was because he seemed to have a confidence in his own sexuality that few, if any, men of her acquaintance had.

Meagan had been pursued by many men in her life. She knew men found her attractive with her coal-black hair, which she had inherited from her Italian mother, along with her willowy frame and wide mouth. On the other hand, she had inherited her pale complexion, height and arresting green eyes from her Scottish father. It all added up to a combination that drew looks wherever Meagan went, and judging by the admiring looks she was getting from her companion he also found the combination to his liking. But although Meagan was conscious of the effect she had on men, she had little time for love affairs. She had her future mapped out and nothing and no one was going to stand in the way of her achieving her dreams.

But until that night no other man had made her feel as if she wanted to give herself up, to lose herself in their arms in the way that he did, despite having just met him. He made her feel that the rest of the world had ceased to exist, as if the future was unimportant, that it was only the here and now that mattered.

And so she went with him along the edge of the shore where the waves lapped at their feet, until they found a place deep in the dunes and hidden from view, where he lowered her gently to the ground. He kissed her eyelids, her ear lobes, and then down to her neck before finding her mouth, kissing her with a hunger that took Meagan's breath away.

Never before had Meagan felt her body respond in such a manner. Almost against her will she arched her body to his, needing to feel the length of his body hard against hers. Suddenly he pulled away.

'You've never made love to a man before, have you?' he said, his voice full of wonder.

Meagan was mortified. Was her lack of experience so obvious? But it was true. She had never, before that night, found a man she wanted to give herself to. She knew when she did finally lose her virginity she wanted it to mean something. She wanted it to be special. And it wasn't as if she'd had many boyfriends. Her studies and her sailing had kept her too busy.

'Its ridiculous, isn't it? A nineteen-year-old virgin in this day and age?' She sat up and hugged her knees.

'Not ridiculous,' he said. 'Kind of wonderful.' He sat next to her and put his arm around her shoulder. '*You're* kind of wonderful,' he said, 'but I think we should get to know one another before we go any further. There will be a right time for us, but it's not yet.' He pulled her back into his arms, and they lay there for the rest of the evening with the feel of the gentle night breeze on their skin. As she told him about her dreams and the sacrifices she'd had to make, he held her and listened. He hadn't said much, only that he too had studied medicine. That he worked in London and was completing his higher training. She never even found out his last name.

And all too soon she had had to leave. The sun was just beginning to make the sky pink and she and her companions were sailing on the high tide.

He held her tightly, kissing her hair and mur-muring endearments.

'Do you have to go? Can't you stay? Now I have found you, I don't want to let you out of my sight. Not even for a minute.'

For a moment she thought about letting them sail without her, but just as quickly dismissed the notion. She was the only one who could safely steer them on the rest of their journey. And somehow she knew there would be time later for her and Cameron.

She kissed him back fiercely.

'I wish I could stay. But we'll see each other soon. You'll come and see me in Edinburgh?'

'The devil himself couldn't stop me,' he said. 'I'll come as soon as I can. In the meantime, take care. Watch the seas around here.' Then he kissed her and she clung to him, unwilling to leave. Only the knowledge that she would see him soon gave her the strength to walk away from him. But she had been wrong. Despite his promises he had never come.

* * *

Aware that he was waiting for a response, Meagan dragged her thoughts back to the present.

'Of course. It was a long time ago. We were both a lot younger then. I was only nineteen. I'm sure we've both had a few "meetings" since then.'

That wasn't strictly true. Since Cameron, there had only been Charlie. And even with Charlie it had never been quite like that night with Cameron. She had put it down to first love, making herself believe that nothing and no one could ever measure up to the intensity of believing yourself in love for the first time. And that's all it had been, she told herself firmly. An impressionable teenager's first real experience of love. It wasn't altogether surprising she had never really forgotten him…

'Shall we get back?' Cameron said abruptly, looking over her shoulder into the distance. 'It feels like its going to rain.'

They walked back down the hill in silence. Meagan wondered what Cameron was thinking. Was he glad that they had met again? Or was he dismayed to find that they'd be working together? She sneaked glances at him, but she couldn't tell anything from his expression.

As they reached the front of the building,

Meagan could make out the slim figure of Rachel leaning against Cameron's car, watching them. A young dark-haired boy was kicking a football nearby.

'Cameron, Meagan. You're back,' Rachel called out as they approached. Although she smiled, Meagan thought she didn't look very pleased. 'Cameron, what have you being doing, dragging our new doctor over these muddy fields? I'm sure she has better things to do.'

'I loved seeing it. It's so beautiful here. Besides, Cameron leant me a pair of wellington boots from the house,' Meagan said. 'I hope they didn't belong to anyone.'

Rachel dismissed her comments with a wave of a manicured hand. 'That's quite all right,' she said. 'Help yourself any time. The house keeps a selection for visitors. No, I just wondered if Cameron would be joining us for lunch. You're welcome to stay too, Meagan, of course.' Meagan was surprised when Rachel said 'us' in that emphasizing way. What could she mean? What exactly did she have to do with Grimsay House? She certainly seemed to have a proprietorial air about her.

Just then the small boy came running over.

'Daddy, will you play football with me? Mummy says she can't and Effie is still in bed. Please, Daddy?'

CHAPTER THREE

STUNNED, Meagan looked at Cameron and then at the young boy. The resemblance was there in the dark hair and full lips, although the child had his mother's eyes. So Cameron and Rachel were together—what on earth did he think he had been playing at a little while ago? Stroking her arm, mentioning their night together? Meagan felt her heart plummet. Somehow she had always thought herself still a little bit in love with Cameron's memory and now it was sullied forever. With sickening clarity she realised he was just like Charlie.

'Meagan, I'd like you to meet my son, Ian. Ian, this is Dr Galbraith.'

'Happy to meet you,' Ian said, holding out his hand to Meagan. His serious expression and behaviour was that of a much older child. She shook his hand gravely.

'Nice to meet you,' she said pleased her voice sounded steady, but inside her thoughts were whirling around. He was married? To Rachel? And a *son*. Why hadn't he said anything? Had he been married back then? If so, what a fool she had been. No wonder he didn't seem to want her here.

'I am pleased to meet you too,' the young boy said formally.

'And you've met my ex-wife, Rachel?'

Rachel smiled enigmatically. 'Oh, this is just a temporary blip, darling,' she drawled. 'As soon as you see sense and come back to London, everything will be back as it should be.'

Cameron frowned. He indicated Ian with a tip of his head. 'Not now, Rachel,' he said, his voice a river of steel. The tension between him and Rachel was palpable. He turned to the young boy, who was looking anxiously from one to the other. 'I can't play with you just now, *mo ghaol*, but I promise to after lunch. Deal?'

'What about Dr Galbraith?' Ian asked. 'Is she going to stay for lunch? I could show her my den.' He turned to Meagan, looking up at her with soulful brown eyes. 'My daddy told me the new doctor is a good sailor. I love going out on boats. Can I go out with you?'

'I would love to take you out sailing one day,' Meagan replied, laughing. 'And I would love to see your den. But I have to go right now, so maybe another time?'

The young boy nodded, satisfied, before running off to continue his game. As she looked after him, she felt her heart squeeze. At one time she'd thought she would be the mother of just such a little boy.

Her mind racing with the turn events had taken, all Meagan wanted was to put as much distance as possible between her and the couple in front of her. She needed time to think.

Rachel hooked her slim arm in Cameron's with an easy familiarity. 'Cameron,' she said, smiling into his eyes, 'I do hope you've invited Meagan to the ball. We could do with a new face to liven things up.'

'Jessie did mention a ball earlier,' Meagan said. 'Thank you for the invitation, but I'm afraid I'll have to decline. If Cameron is going—which I am sure he is—then I'll be on call. Besides, I didn't bring anything suitable to wear.'

'Oh, don't worry about dresses. I've got plenty. You'd be more than welcome to take your pick. Although—' she eyed Meagan's figure critically '—they might need some adjusting. Mrs MacLeod is pretty good with a needle.'

Cheek, Meagan thought furiously. Just because Rachel didn't have an ounce of fat on her!

'Don't worry, Meagan, the whole practice will be there. Everyone is looking forward to it.' Cameron spoke before Meagan could formulate another refusal.

But Rachel, considering the discussion closed, moved on. She smiled seductively up at Cameron. 'Ian is so looking forward to spending some time with his daddy *and* mummy,' Rachel said, reaching up to Cameron and touching his cheek with a long finger. 'And so am I.' Without waiting for a reply, she turned and sashayed back to the house.

Cameron watched her go, his expression inscrutable.

Meagan turned to Cameron. 'I'm not really expected to go to this ball, am I?'

'Yep, sorry. Doctor's orders. It will give you the chance to mix with locals and dignitaries alike. Colin thinks it's good public relations for everyone to attend—the whole practice will be there. Colin and his wife should be back for it, if it makes you feel better.'

Meagan felt annoyed at the cavalier manner with which he seemed to be arranging her social life. But was it just that? she wondered. She felt angry with him for not mentioning his marriage or child. But it wasn't as if it was any of her business. Likewise, what she did in her spare time was her own affair.

'What gives you the right to accept invitations on my behalf?'

'I'm sorry. But I'm afraid you'll just have to accept that on a small island such as this, to refuse an invitation is to give offence.'

Meagan bristled. It was on the tip of her tongue to tell him to go to hell, but she swallowed her annoyance. He was her boss after all.

'Very well,' she conceded. 'If you put it like that, I suppose I can't refuse.'

'Good, that's settled, then. Would you like to stay for lunch?'

'No, if I am allowed to refuse any invitations at all, I'd rather not. I've still to unpack.'

'Of course you don't have to stay for lunch. It's perfectly understandable that you have things to do. I'll see you tomorrow, then. Eight-thirty? I can give you a quick tour and a rundown of the patients before surgery.' He spoke calmly, politely, as if they were perfect strangers, which Meagan supposed they were.

Before she had a chance to reply, he turned on his heel and crossed over to his son. Laughing, he swooped him into his arms and tossed him into the air. With the sound of delighted childish giggles ringing in her ears, Meagan started walking back to her house, realising as she did so that she had left her medical bag and boots at the house. Loath to face Cameron or Rachel again until she had time to get her emotions under control, she decided that she would collect them later.

Stomping down the road to her cottage, she noticed an elderly female figure dressed in a tweed suit and headscarf coming towards her.

'Good morning!' the woman greeted her. 'I thought I'd look in on you on my way to getting the church ready for evening service.' A gnarled hand was offered. 'I'm the housekeeper—Mrs

McLeod, but call me Flora. We don't hold much with ceremony here. Welcome to Uist—I hope you'll be happy here.'

'Oh, Mrs McLeod—Flora. Nice to meet you. Thank you for the fire and provisions you left last night. You've no idea how welcome they were.'

'Aye, I heard you'd got yourself into a bit of difficulty on the road,' Flora said, with a suspicious gleam in her eye.

'Oh, no!' Meagan said, dismayed. 'Is it all round the island already?' So much for making a good impression, she thought, her heart sinking a little.

'I'm afraid that everyone will be interested in the new doctor from the mainland. Apart from summer visitors, we don't get many new faces coming to live here. It's bound to be the main topic of conversation after church today. How the new doctor tried to kill herself and half the island and then needed to be rescued.' Flora gave a little chuckle, clearly highly amused by the previous day's events.

'Yes, I realise now that it was Dr Stuart—Lord Grimsay. Although at the time he looked more like a fisherman.' Meagan remarked unsure how she was supposed to refer to Cameron.

Flora's mouth tightened and a coolness entered her eyes.

'You mean you thought he looked too ordinary? Well, we don't keep with people giving themselves airs and graces here.'

Obviously the local population thought highly of Cameron, Meagan thought, remembering the easy teasing between him and the bystanders the day before.

Realising that she might have put her foot in it and anxious to make amends, Meagan offered Flora a cup of tea.

'No, thanks, dear, not today. But I'll pop by tomorrow to give things in the house a bit of going over. Dr MacDonald has arranged for me to come in for a couple of hours three days a week, if that suits you?'

Meagan really didn't want someone in the house, tidying up after her, but it would be rude and churlish to refuse. They parted, agreeing that the arrangement would continue as agreed.

Meagan spent the rest of the afternoon unpacking and settling into her new home. As she found places for her clothes and books, her thoughts kept returning to Cameron. *Had* he already been married that night? If so, then he had behaved unforgivably and was no better than Charlie. How old was Ian? Meagan hadn't had much experience with children but she thought he was about five or six. It was just over six years since that night, so Rachel must have been pregnant then or at least soon after. What was it about men? Meagan thought furiously. At least the men she seemed to fall for. If she'd thought that Cameron was different, she had been badly mistaken.

Still, it was better to find out sooner rather than later. Now she knew just exactly what sort of man she was dealing with, she'd be on her guard. She had to work with Cameron, and they had to get along as colleagues, but apart from that she'd keep her distance.

The next day dawned with a change in the weather. The wind had risen, bringing with it rain that hurled itself against the windows of Meagan's car. As she drove to the surgery, she was glad of her vehicle's efficient heater.

She had dressed carefully in a well-cut beige

linen trouser suit, ruefully aware that it was probably a tad too dressy. Just before she left the house, she removed her wedding ring and placed it safely in a drawer. As she had told Cameron, she wanted this to be a new start. It was time to break her last, final link with Charlie.

She was scheduled to help Cameron with the morning clinic and then accompany him on visits in the afternoon. If she had time, she would include a return visit to the big house to see how Effie was getting on, although she was pretty certain Jessie would have called if there hadn't been an improvement.

As she drove, her thoughts turned to Cameron and the feelings he had stirred up. She was still attracted to him, she couldn't deny it, and her attraction unsettled her. But looking on the bright side, maybe it meant she was getting over Charlie. Yes, she was still vulnerable and raw. Thinking of his death still pained her but no longer in the way that it had once done. She was even able to accept that some of the blame attached to the deterioration of their marriage might lie with her.

She had been an exceptionally driven medical

student and junior doctor. When she hadn't been working the long hours demanded by her training, she had been studying hard for her exams. And that had left little time for her and Charlie. In the early years of their marriage he had often tried to arrange outings for them both: nights out to the theatre and restaurants—walking trips in the Scottish hills. Things that had initially drawn them together. But increasingly she had declined to go with him, pleading the pressures of work and study. And so eventually he had gone by himself and she guessed that that had been how he had eventually met and fallen in love with Catherine. And she had never even suspected. What was she? A trusting fool? Or too wrapped up in her own career? One thing was for sure, however, she may be attracted to Cameron and getting over Charlie, but that didn't mean she was ready for a relationship. She smiled to herself. Wasn't she getting a bit ahead of herself? There was nothing to indicate that Cameron wanted anything more from her than a professional relationship. Besides, he looked like a man who liked playing the field. And then there was Rachel. There was still something between them, that much was obvious.

She was still chewing over the problem when she arrived at the surgery. She was looking forward to getting started and hoped it would be a full day, the busier the better. Working hard left less time for brooding.

She found that most of the staff had arrived ahead of her. Cameron, dressed in a dark grey suit with a striped tie, welcomed her formally. If possible, he looked even more good-looking and her heart gave a traitorous flip.

'I thought we'd start with a tour before morning surgery starts,' he said. 'You have a small number of patients to see. I thought we'd ease you in gently.' He gave her a crooked smile.

Meagan had already seen the waiting area and the meeting room but Cameron showed her around the clinical areas. Apart from three examination rooms there was a separate treatment room for minor procedures.

'We do all our own minor surgery here,' Cameron explained. 'As Colin said, anything complicated we either send to Stornoway or, if more serious, to Glasgow. There is an air ambulance for emergency transfers, but occasionally we have no choice but to operate at the small local hospital. It's equipped for most emergencies. How are your surgical skills anyway?'

'Fortunately or unfortunately, depending on which way you look at it, that was one area where I got a lot of experience while I was working abroad,' Meagan replied with a smile.

'I must impress on you, Meagan, that you should always seek to use the expert facilities whenever possible. If you have any doubt, please call me for advice. We do not want you thinking you are back in the field and able to perform inappropriate procedures on our patients.'

Stung by his remarks, Meagan felt her smile freeze and her temper rise. Where was the easy-going man from yesterday? It seemed he was keen to ensure that she knew that now they were working together, he was the boss.

'I can assure you, Cameron, I have no intention of carrying out procedures for which I am neither as equipped nor as qualified as others close to hand. I was simply trying to reassure you that I can cope, if need be, in an emergency situation,' she replied, her voice clipped with the effort of keeping it under control.

She couldn't make head or tail of this man. One

minute he was friendly, the next he was treating her as if she was a belligerent medical student.

'Good,' Cameron replied brusquely. 'Just as long as you realise that top marks in examinations and a couple of years' experience in a third-world situation is not enough to make a competent GP. Hands-on experience in the field of general practice is what counts.'

'What exactly is bothering you about me being here?' Meagan asked with an exasperated lift of her eyebrow. 'The fact that I did very well in my exams or that I am not very experienced? May I remind you that I have completed several years of medical training and my full general practice rotation, and that neither the General Medical Council nor Dr MacDonald seem to have any reservations regarding my suitability to practise.'

'I'm sure that you are eminently qualified Meagan.' Cameron's voice was soft. 'Of your academic ability there can be no doubt. I am simply anxious that you don't overreach yourself. Shall we leave it at that for the time being?' He smiled his lovely smile which softened his face. 'Come, I'll show you the rest of the place. Then we'll get going.'

As it turned out the day was as busy as Meagan had hoped. She had a large number of patients allocated to her, although she suspected that the more serious or complex cases had been sifted out by Cameron as all the patients were suffering from either minor viral illnesses or simply needed reassurance.

'You will give me a shout if there is anything you're not sure of?' he had said at the start of the clinic. Meagan had bitten her tongue and had reassured him that she would. She would just have to let time take its course and he would eventually come to trust her medical skills.

After morning surgery, Cameron introduced her to the rest of the team. There was Sophie, a woman near retiring age, who was the practice nurse, and the health visitor, Dorothy, a kindly-looking woman in her early thirties. Both women welcomed Meagan warmly and she looked forward to working with them. Apart from the nursing staff there was a receptionist called Mary, who looked as if she had worked there for ever. Meagan suspected she ruled the place with a rod of iron.

They all had lunch together in the small staff-room at the back of the surgery. Dorothy told Meagan that they tried to have lunch together whenever possible. Dr MacDonald and Dr Stuart liked knowing that everyone was up to date with what was happening to their patients. Eventually the conversation turned to Meagan's visit to Grimsay House.

'So you met young Effie and her mum Jessie, then? And did you meet the glamorous Rachel?' said Dorothy with a pointed glance at Cameron, which he studiously ignored. 'Is everything OK with Effie? Would you like me to pop in and see them this afternoon?'

As well as being responsible, along with the medical staff, for the antenatal care of women on the island, Dorothy also had responsibility for the under fives as well as the elderly. Cameron had told her that small rural practices could rarely afford to employ more than one health visitor so, unlike their counterparts in the cities who tended to specialise in only one of these areas, health visitors like Dorothy had to combine the three roles.

'That's OK, but thanks anyway, Dorothy,' said Meagan with a warm smile. 'I'd prefer to go myself, as I promised Jessie that I would call. I'll go after I finish visits with you, Cameron, if that suits you?'

Cameron nodded.

Dorothy looked a little relieved. 'I've got a few other calls I want to make so one less would help. Actually, I got a call just before lunch from Katie White. She's feeling a little anxious, Cameron. Thinks the baby hasn't being moving as much as he has been. I said I would go and see her after lunch.'

Cameron looked thoughtful. 'How many weeks pregnant is she?' he asked Dorothy, holding his hand out for the notes that Dorothy held in her lap.

'Thirty-six. Just. She's due to be admitted to Stornoway in two weeks.'

Meagan looked enquiringly at Cameron.

'Katie White is 33 and pregnant with her first child. Like almost all the mothers here, she'll be sent either to Lewis or to Glasgow a couple of weeks in advance of delivery. Even earlier if it looks like there might be a problem. Obviously it's not ideal, especially for women like Katie whose husband is a commercial diver and can't afford to take time off work to stay with her in Stornoway, but it is believed to be safer for mother and child. We try to keep them at home as long as we safely can. Katie has had a normal pregnancy to date and I'm not anticipating any problems. It's good that you're going to see her, Dorothy. Meagan and I will be on visits ourselves but you can reach us on my mobile if you have any concerns. Speaking of which, we should be on our way. C'mon, Meagan. We'll take my car. I'll just get my bag and the notes.'

As they headed off towards their first visit, Meagan bit her lip, trying to find the right words. She needed to ask him about Rachel.

Taking a breath to steady her voice, she turned to him. 'Cameron, that night—back then—were you married?'

He kept on driving, concentrating on the road. A muscle twitched in his cheek.

'No,' he said. 'I'm not the sort of man who would be with another woman if I was married. No matter how strong the temptation.' He slid a look in Meagan's direction and she was annoyed to find herself blushing.

'But,' he said, 'I had been seeing Rachel before

I met you. We had broken up a couple of weeks before. And then, the day I returned to London, she came to see me. She was pregnant and there was no doubt the child was mine. I thought…' He broke off, shaking his head. 'It doesn't matter now what I thought. We got married. We had a son, and now we are divorced.' His tone was clipped. A spasm of pain crossed his features.

Meagan wanted to know more, but something in his expression warned her not to probe. His marriage and subsequent divorce clearly caused him pain. No doubt he was still in love with his ex-wife. How could he not be? She was so beautiful. She decided to let the matter drop. Let the past stay there. She and Cameron were different people now, work colleagues and perhaps in the future friends. That was all she wanted. Wasn't it?

The first patient lived fairly close to the surgery. He was an elderly man suffering from shortness of breath. No doubt he could have managed to come to the surgery, albeit with difficulty. He and his wife apologised for the trouble they were putting the doctors to. And not just one but two!

They shook their heads in amazement. Cameron was quick to reassure them.

'It's no trouble. That's what we're here for. There's two of us as it's Dr Galbraith's first day and I wanted to show her where everyone lives. You know it's not easy to find some of the houses here. And as for us coming to see you, I'll not have you coming to see us on a wet and miserable day such as this. Particularly when you're feeling low. And especially when I know that there's every chance of tea and home baking,' he said casting a hopeful eye at Mr Morrison's wife.

'As if we'd let you leave this house without your *strupack*,' Mrs Morrison admonished, wagging a gnarled finger. 'I'll just get it ready while you're seeing to John.'

As she bustled out of the bedroom Cameron explained the patient's history.

'Mr Morrison here is 75 years old. He was fit and well up until a couple of days ago when he developed shortness of breath.' He stood back to allow Meagan to examine the older man who was sitting up in bed, looking drawn and flushed.

'There's nothing wrong with me,' he protested a little grumpily. 'It's that wife of mine. She just fusses. I've got work to do, but she won't let me out of bed long enough to see to it.'

Meagan caught Cameron's eye and smiled briefly.

'We'll just give you a quick look-over, if that's all right? Better to be safe than sorry, eh?'

She listened to his chest and examined his ankles for swelling. Then she took his temperature, which was elevated.

'It looks like a chest infection, Mr Morrison. It's not serious, but I'm surprised you're even considering getting out of bed and going out on the croft. You must be feeling pretty lousy.'

'I suppose I'm not feeling that great, but someone has to see to the animals. Anyway, a bit of flu never killed anyone.'

'I'm afraid a chest infection at your age can turn nasty,' Meagan said gently. 'I do think you need to take it easy for a while, take plenty of fluids, and I'll prescribe you some antibiotics. If you follow my advice we should have you back to your usual self in no time.'

'If it's the animals you're worried about I can

ask Donald from the estate to check them for you,' Cameron interjected.

Mr Morrison looked at Meagan then at Cameron.

'I can see that you two have ganged up on me. All right, then,' he conceded. 'If you can ask Donald to check the animals in the top field, I'll do as you say.'

Meagan had some cause to regret that she had bothered with lunch when, after leaving John tucked up in bed, Mrs Morrison ushered them into the sitting room and handed them a plate full of food. There were tiny sandwiches, scones stuffed with cheese and home-made shortbread piled in heaps on the plates. And it was clear that they were expected to eat every bite from the way Mrs Morrison sat herself down in front of them with her arms folded and a satisfied expression on her face.

'Are you not having any yourself?' said Meagan hopefully, holding her plate out to Mrs Morrison.

'Oh, I'm not long after having my lunch,' replied the old lady, rubbing her ample frame. 'And, besides, I have to watch my figure—

unlike some,' she added, eyeing Meagan's slim frame disapprovingly. 'We'll need to get some fat on these bones, won't we, Dr Cameron?'

'Well, you know what young women are like these days, May,' Cameron replied.

Dismayed at the turn the conversation was taking, Meagan was about to make a sharp rejoinder when she noticed that Cameron was having difficulty containing his mirth at her discomfort and, sure enough, when at last, stuffed to the gills, they were able to leave and get on their way to see the next patient, he burst out laughing.

When at last he could eventually speak he said to Meagan, 'I should have warned you about the patients here before you had lunch, but I'm afraid I just couldn't help myself. The same thing happened to me when I first started doing visits, and I knew to refuse hospitality is considered extremely rude, especially by the elderly patients. So I'm afraid it doesn't matter how full you are, you just have to do your best to get it down.'

'I can hardly move,' groaned Meagan

'Well, now you know,' he said, 'Be careful in

future who you visit and when. But as a rule we visit all our elderly sick patients even without a callout. We feel it's an important part of the service here.' He went on, 'And it has practical advantages too. It means that we can keep an eye on things and often prevent minor ailments turning into something more serious. I just hope you don't find it all a little boring for you,' he teased.

'I really like the way you look after the patients here,' Meagan assured him. 'Even going as far as sorting his worries about the croft out for him. Where would you see that in an urban practice?' She smiled at Cameron. 'I know GPs in busy inner-city practices who hardly ever get to see the same patient twice. I much prefer to get to know my patients. What makes them tick, what worries them. It's one of the reasons I wanted to work in a rural practice.'

'On the downside, it means that we get very involved with them,' Cameron said. 'Sometimes it's harder when you know them, but on the whole it's what I like best about living and working here. I've known most of these people all my life.'

They made two other house calls—one to an elderly man with pulmonary oedema and the other to a child with chickenpox. Although both cases were straightforward, Cameron was impressed with the thoroughness with which Meagan examined her patients. She had listened carefully and sympathetically as they outlined her symptoms and she had a relaxed and friendly manner, which put the patients immediately at their ease. It was clear to Cameron that she was going to prove a popular member of the team and he felt himself beginning to relax.

Having diplomatically escaped the offer of refeshments from the harassed young mother, Meagan asked, 'Who is next on our list?'

'Robert McLean. He lives close to the Benbecula side. He's our furthest-away call. The last two we'll see on the way back to the surgery.' Suddenly he slowed the car down to a crawl.

'Hello, what's this? Dorothy's car is still at Katie White's house. I would have expected her to have been on her way by now.' A small frown creased his brow. 'Let's just pop in while we are passing.'

As he swung the car into the driveway a very anxious-looking Dorothy came out of the house.

'Thank goodness you're here. I tried your mobile a couple of times but you must have been in a dead spot as I couldn't get a response.'

'What is it, Dorothy? What's wrong?'

'I thought I'd listen to the foetal heart to reassure Katie, but her instincts seem right. The baby's heartbeat is very slow. Around 50. I've also done a brief examination and there's worse. Her waters have broken and I can see the cord. I'm afraid we are dealing with a cord prolapse and a very distressed baby.'

Meagan felt a flutter of anxiety. She knew from her obstetric experience that this was bad news for mother and baby. Particularly as they were so far away from a hospital with the specialist obstetric and paediatric facilities such a situation required. Despite Cameron having qualified as a paediatrician, the baby, if it survived, would need admission to a high-dependency unit.

'When I couldn't reach you, I took the liberty of phoning the air ambulance. They are on standby, awaiting your call,' Dorothy went on, calmer now that her colleagues had arrived.

Pretty certain that Dorothy would be correct in

her diagnosis, Cameron knew they would have to act quickly if the baby was to have any chance of survival. Putting his own anxieties aside at the thought of dealing with a premature distressed baby, he said, 'It'll take at least two hours to get mother and baby to Glasgow. We won't have that long if we are to save the mother. We'll need to get her delivered. Meagan, have you performed an emergency section before?'

'Yes, many times. But always in a proper theatre. Are you suggesting we perform one here?'

'There is a proper theatre in the local hospital which is ten minutes from here. It's normally reserved for minor procedures but, as I told you this morning, it is fully equipped for emergencies such as this. Dr Lake, one of the Benbecula GPs, is qualified to act as an anaesthetist if we need one.'

Making up his mind, he turned to Dorothy and Meagan. 'We don't have time to wait for the air ambulance. If mother and baby are to stand a chance, we need to deliver the baby straight away. I'll speak to Katie. Meagan, phone Ambulance Control and tell them what we are planning to do. They'll need to come to evacuate mother and, hopefully, baby to Glasgow anyway. The surgery will patch you through. Dorothy, get hold of Dr Lake and get him to meet us at the hospital. Then phone the hospital and tell them to prepare the theatre. We'll take Katie in my car. In the meantime, I'll insert a catheter into Katie's bladder to fill it. That'll help keep the pressure off the cord and should buy us some time. Quickly, everyone. Time is critical.' And before Meagan could say anything else, he disappeared inside the house.

Meagan and Dorothy looked at each other for one horror-struck moment before swinging into action. Tasks completed, they helped a terrified Katie into the car.

The young mother looked from Meagan to Cameron. She clutched at Meagan's hand. 'You've got to save my baby. I can't lose this child. Promise me you'll do everything you can. And, please, find Neil. I need him.'

By the time they arrived at the hospital Dr Lake had everything in place to perform the operation. Cameron and Meagan scrubbed up together while Dorothy kept an eye on the baby's heartbeat.

'Cameron, how many Caesareans have you carried out in the last two years?' Meagan asked.

'None,' Cameron replied. 'I did a few when I was a senior house officer. But I guess that was some time ago,' he admitted.

'I should do it, then,' said Meagan firmly. 'I've carried out tons in the last year and while I'd rather not be doing one here under these conditions, I think that I should do the procedure. Besides, you're the one with paediatric experience and I have very little. You are going to have to work on that baby the moment it's delivered.'

'I can't let you do it, Meagan. I made the decision to operate and if anything goes wrong, it will be my responsibility.'

'Oh, for God's sake, get off your high horse. The responsibility lies with both of us. Dangerous or not, I agree with you completely. If we are going to save them, we need to operate. And the best chance we have of pulling them through is for me to do the procedure and for you to stand by to resuscitate the baby if need be. Agreed?'

Cameron could tell when he was beaten. Besides, he could see that what Meagan was saying made perfect sense. He would have to trust her operating capabilities, just as she had trusted him enough to go along with his decision in the first place. And they didn't have time to argue.

'Well, then, what are we waiting for? Let's go,' he said with a swift smile backing into the theatre.

Katie lay on the theatre table. Dr Lake bent over her, ready to administer the anaesthetic. She looked frightened and sought Cameron's eyes for reassurance.

'You and baby will be fine,' he promised. 'We'll be transferring you both to Glasgow once we've finished here. I'll travel with you and see you settled. We've managed to locate Neil and he's on his way.'

Slowly Katie's eyes closed as she succumbed to the anaesthetic. Meagan took a deep breath and in response to a quick nod from Cameron made a deep, sure incision across Katie's abdomen. Within a matter of minutes she had cut through the protective sac that held the baby and gently lifted it into Cameron's waiting arms. 'A little girl,' Cameron informed the room. 'And not a bad size, considering she's early.'

The baby looked blue and was unresponsive.

Cameron quickly cleared the tiny girl's mouth of any mucus that might be clogging her airway. Precious seconds ticked past but the baby's heartbeat remained slow.

'I'll have to intubate,' Cameron said quietly, and quickly inserted a small tube into the baby's windpipe before attaching an ambu-bag to breathe air into the baby's lungs. Dorothy rested her hand gently over the baby's chest. 'The heartbeat is improving and she's pinking up nicely,' she announced to everyone's relief. 'I think she's going to be fine.'

Cameron removed the tube and moments later the welcome sound of a baby's cry filled the theatre, causing a collective sigh of relief.

Meagan allowed herself a brief moment of pleasure before turning back to work on Katie. It was important as she sewed her up to ensure that all vessels that might be bleeding were securely tied off. In many ways this was the trickiest part of the procedure.

It was another thirty minutes before Meagan stood back, and peeling off her gloves, said with satisfaction, 'Katie'll be fine. She's beginning to come round. Hopefully the air ambulance will be here by the time she wakes up so we can transfer her straight away. How's the baby?'

'She's fine. But the sooner she gets to the special care baby unit in Glasgow the happier I'll be. She's going to need some intensive nursing for the next few days, but the biggest danger's past. Nicely done, everyone.' Cameron smiled his relief at Meagan. 'Particularly you, Dr Galbraith. Welcome to the team.'

Katie, coming around from the anaesthetic, opened her eyes and, although still very sleepy, was alert enough to know that everything had gone well.

'Thank you,' she whispered, her eyes fixed on her baby

'We're not out of the woods yet,' Cameron warned her, 'but I suspect that in a short while we'll be welcoming you and baby home. '

'The air ambulance is here. And Neil has just arrived,' called Dorothy, who had left theatre to investigate. Meagan felt the tension leave her body. The quicker mother and baby were safely in Glasgow, the better. As soon as the crew from the air ambulance were ready with their stretcher, they transferred Katie and wheeled her out to the waiting aircraft. Meagan followed them with the warmly wrapped newborn, who had been placed in an incubator. Cameron settled his patients, ensuring he had easy access to them both should they require help during the short flight. Within minutes the plane was making its final preparations for take-off.

'Meagan, you'll have to take the on-call tonight until I get back. In the meantime, if there are any problems, give one of the GPs in the other practice a shout. They'll be glad to help. Won't they, Dr Lake?' he said over his shoulder. 'I should be back in a few hours.'

And with a flurry of activity the plane took off with the small family for its return journey to Glasgow.

Once Meagan had written up her notes, she left the hospital. Before he left, Cameron had suggested that she leave the remaining visits until the next day as there wasn't anything that couldn't wait and it was now well after five o'clock.

However, Meagan thought that she would call on Effie as she knew that Jessie would be expecting her. After all, Grimsay House was on her way home. She would pop in on her way back from the surgery after she'd written up the notes on the other patients they'd seen that afternoon.

Jessie had heeded Meagan's advice and kept Effie in bed for a second day, although, judging by the child's high spirits, she was going to be up and about as soon as she could. Like the day before, Jessie insisted that Meagan follow her to the kitchen for tea and 'a wee bite to eat'. It was on the tip of her tongue to refuse, but she remembered what Cameron had said earlier in the day. Besides, she enjoyed Jessie's easy company.

'Well, Meagan—Dr Galbraith—you've certainly made an impact on your first few days on our island!' Jessie said as she buttered pancakes. 'First your near miss on the road and then saving the life of Katie White's new baby. The phone lines were hot when the air ambulance was spotted arriving. We haven't had this much excitement on the island since Donald Bhan's bull chased a hapless tourist last year. I think I'm going to like having you around,' Jessie chuckled.

Meagan smiled ruefully. 'I keep forgetting how quickly news spreads on the island. Yes, we were lucky with Mrs White's baby but that's our job. It shouldn't be made more of than that.'

'Oh, don't be so modest. Everyone says you and Cameron made a fantastic team. We are very lucky to have you here.'

'Thanks Jessie,' Meagan replied, deciding to accept the praise with good grace. 'But, please, call me Meagan. And, besides, you are right— it was a team effort. Cameron really is an excellent doctor. The island is lucky to have someone with his level of experience with children here.'

'And good-looking, too,' Jessie added with a teasing look at Meagan.

'Is he? I can't say I noticed,' Meagan lied, hoping that a tell-tale blush wasn't staining her cheeks. The last thing she needed or wanted was speculation about her and Cameron.

'Please, don't get any ideas Jessie,' she continued, more sharply than she had intended. 'Cameron and I are colleagues and apart from the fact that I'm not looking for romance, I happen to think it's a bad idea for colleagues to get involved. Anyway, I very much doubt if I am the kind of woman to interest Dr Stuart,' she finished with a fleeting smile. 'And what's more, he and Rachel still seem involved.'

'Ah, Cameron and Rachel. I guess you know that they were married. And that Ian's their son?'

'They still seem to be a couple. Doesn't she still live here?' Meagan tried hard to keep the curiosity from her voice.

'Rachel lives in London most of the time. Ian lives here, with his father. Rachel comes back every couple of weeks to see Ian and naturally she stays here. There is no shortage of space after all.'

'Why doesn't Ian live with his mother?' Meagan asked. 'Wouldn't that be the usual arrangement?'

'Cameron feels he can provide a more stable environment for him here. Mrs MacLeod and I help look after him when Cameron's at work. And, besides, all this will be Ian's one day. It's right that he's brought up here. And anyway…' She bit her lip as if she had started to say something and then changed her mind. 'Hey, I thought you weren't interested in Cameron.' She grinned at Meagan.

'I'm not,' Meagan protested. Then, feeling as if she had been too forceful, she added, 'Or at any rate, only to the extent anyone is interested in the people they work with. But, yes, let's talk about something else. You, for instance.'

Apart from a perceptive look at Meagan, Jessie wisely changed the subject.

As they chatted like old friends, they arranged to meet up for a bar supper one evening. Jessie would get her mother to look after Effie so that she could enjoy a rare night out.

Meagan eventually returned home around eight that evening. She had wanted to ensure that all the notes were up to date and that the nurses had an opportunity to tell her about any patients who might call her out that night. Despite Cameron telling her that he'd take over the on-call when he returned from Glasgow, Meagan was sure he'd be too tired and had instructed the staff to direct all emergencies to her. She had also had to make a call on a young woman who had a suspected fracture. Meagan had dispatched her by road to the hospital for an X-ray and the cast that Meagan was confident she'd require.

She had just finished stoking up the fire and warming up the pan of stew with dumplings that Mrs Macleod had left for her when there was a knock on the door. Meagan opened it to find Cameron leaning against the doorframe. As she had suspected he was exhausted. Lines of tiredness etched his face.

Noticing her anxious appraisal of him and thinking it related to Katie, Cameron was quick to reassure Meagan. 'I thought I'd call on my way home to let you know that mother and baby are doing well,' he said, smiling his lopsided grin, 'and to pick up the on-call report.' He sniffed the air appreciatively. 'Let me guess. Mrs MacLeod's famous stew and dumplings?'

'You guessed right. Please, won't you join me? You couldn't have had anything to eat for hours,' Meagan offered, keen to build on the camaraderie that they appeared to be establishing.

'Now, that's an offer I can't refuse,' said Cameron, stepping through to the tiny kitchen. His broad frame seemed to fill the room. 'Knowing Flora, she'll have made enough to feed an army. And I am ravenous.'

As they sat and ate, they chatted comfortably about the day's events. Having informed him she would remain on call for the night, Meagan brought him up to date on the evening surgery and the patient that she had sent to hospital.

As they drank their coffee they chatted companionably about work and Meagan found herself telling him about her experiences with Médecins Sans Frontières.

'Of course,' she admitted, 'it wasn't all success stories. We lost many patients we shouldn't have, either through lack equipment or through lack of proper experience.' Memories of the patients' they had lost caused her eyes to fill momentarily with tears and she missed the look of compassion in Cameron's eyes.

Cameron was finding the mixture of enthusiasm and sadness in the young woman who sat across from him aroused feelings that he hadn't known for a long time. She was unaware that the passion she felt for her work showed in her face and gestures as she talked animatedly about her time abroad.

He also knew what it was like to lose a patient to inexperience. Even if that inexperience hadn't been his, he had still felt responsible.

Almost without knowing what he was doing, he leant across and gently brushed a tear from her face. He'd like to banish the sadness from this woman's eyes.

Cameron watched as the conflicting emotions chased themselves across Meagan's face. Despite himself, he was still powerfully attracted to her. Mesmerised, he reached over to her and pulled her up and against him. For a long moment they gazed deeply into each other's eyes before Cameron stood up and, muttering something in Gaelic, pulled her towards him, cupping her chin in one hand while tracing the contours of her mouth with the slender fingers of his other hand. Suddenly with a groan he covered her mouth with his, gently at first then, as he felt her response, more urgently. She felt his body grow hard with desire and she moulded her body to his. Time seem to stand still as they explored each other's bodies with their mouths and hands. Cameron let his hands travel over her breasts down to encircle her narrow waist before they came to rest on her hips, pulling her ever closer. The part of Meagan's mind that was still rational was shocked, but the other part had long ago thrown caution to the wind. All she wanted at that moment was for Cameron not to stop but to possess her completely, extinguishing the last shred of the hurt of Charlie's betrayal.

Just then the shrill sound of the telephone cut through the air. Cameron released her reluctantly and for a moment they stood looking at each other and breathing deeply. Cameron's eyes glowed almost black with passion

'You better get that,' Cameron suggested. 'It could be someone looking for the on-call doctor.'

Still a little dazed, Meagan answered the phone.

It was a patient, complaining of a sore foot. Meagan offered to visit but the patient, a man in his early forties, was adamant that she wasn't to put herself out. He'd be happy, he reassured her, if he could come and see her the next day at the surgery. And really he wouldn't have called at all if his wife hadn't made him.

Satisfied that she had done all she could, Meagan advised some painkillers to help him sleep. 'Come and see me at the surgery to-morrow,' she said, then ended the call.

When Meagan returned to the sitting room Cameron was standing, hands deep in his pockets, looking distant.

'Who was it?' he asked, his voice cool.

'Someone complaining of a sore foot. I've arranged to see him at the surgery tomorrow. A Mr McLean.' Meagan was puzzled by the change in Cameron.

'Robert McLean?' Cameron asked sharply. 'From Howbeg?'

'Yes,' Meagan replied. 'Do you know him?'

Cameron looked thoughtful. 'Robert MacLean. The patient we didn't make it to today. He has a long history of unstable diabetes. He rarely calls the doctor out but when he does it usually means that it's something quite serious.' He frowned. 'Really, Meagan, you should have taken a more detailed history over the phone or at the very least passed the call to me.'

Meagan was dismayed and hurt by his attitude. OK, she probably should have taken a more detailed history, but the patient had seemed reluctant for her to visit and had seemed satisfied to see her the next morning. Cameron's annoyance seemed out of proportion to the situation.

'If I had known he had a history of diabetes, of course I would have gone to see him. In fact,' she said 'I'll go and see him now.'

'No, I'll go. I think its better—don't you? And in future please take the time to read the notes of patients before making a decision whether or not to visit.'

Meagan could hardly believe that the man in front of her was the same man who only a short time ago had been making love to her. What on earth had got into her? Hadn't she only hours before promised herself that she would keep him at a distance? And, as far as she knew, there was still something between him and Rachel. She had let this man tramp all over her feelings once before, and it seemed as if he was quite prepared to do so again—if she let him.

'I'm sorry,' she said stiffly. 'It won't happen again.' She knew that he knew she wasn't just referring to the patient.

'And, Meagan—' he turned towards her as he made to leave '—I think it would be better if we both forgot about what just happened here. Please, forgive me—I had no right.'

Meagan felt herself grow warm with humiliation. Clearly he regretted his lapse in self-control as well as continuing to harbour reservations about her medical abilities.

Well, more fool her for believing that he was different. She wouldn't make that mistake again in a hurry. She would never let him, or any man, catch her off guard again, she vowed silently.

She held the door open. 'At least we agree on something. It most certainly was a mistake—I can't imagine what either of us was thinking.' She laughed but it was a mirthless sound. 'Don't worry, I have no intention of repeating tonight so you can relax.'

Cameron hesitated. He could see the hurt reflected in her green eyes. Damn the woman. He wondered if she knew how little she was able to disguise her emotions. He resisted the impulse to reach out and pull her back into his arms. It was better this way. Although he felt more attracted to Meagan than he would have thought possible, she was still vulnerable, and the last thing he wanted to do was take advantage of her susceptibility. If she were any other woman he'd consider having an affair, but she wasn't just any other woman. She had been hurt and he wouldn't be responsible for hurting her again. And he would hurt her. He knew that for certain. Rachel had made it very clear that she wouldn't tolerate him marrying again. She had made it perfectly clear that she would seek custody of Ian if there was even a hint he was interested in another woman. She knew him well enough to know he would never risk losing his son. No, it was far better that Meagan thought him weak and selfish and that they kept their relationship strictly professional.

'Goodnight, then,' he said. 'I'll see you tomorrow.' As Meagan closed the door behind him, he cursed under his breath. How could he have made such a mess of his life?

CHAPTER FOUR

THE next few days were so busy that Meagan had little time to think. If she had ever believed that being a general practitioner on a small island would be an easy option, she had been mistaken. Her surgeries were busy, although Meagan suspected that some of her patients were there just to have a look at the new doctor. But there were plenty of genuine cases to keep her constantly challenged. She didn't see much of Cameron, and when she did he was friendly but distant, and that suited her perfectly.

She was having a quick cup of coffee between patients when the practice nurse came in to see her, her brow puckered with worry.

'Meagan, do you have a moment?' she asked.

'Sure, Sophie. What is it?'

'Could you see someone for me? I've been doing the baby clinic and I noticed that one of the mothers isn't well. She's breathless—more than I'd expect—and I don't know…she just doesn't look right. She says she's been like this for a week or two, and its just flu or something. Dr MacDonald gave her antibiotics when he saw her before he left, but she's no better. She's insisting that she doesn't need to see a doctor but would you mind having a quick look at her for me? I would have asked Cameron, but he's at the hospital. I'm worried if I let her leave without seeing a doctor, she won't come back.'

'Of course, Sophie. Show her in.'

A moment or two later, the nurse ushered in a young exhausted-looking woman in with her baby. Sophie handed Meagan the woman's notes. A quick glance told Meagan that the patient had three children. Her youngest was five months old.

'I'm sorry, Doctor. I don't mean to be a bother. I told Sophie that it was nothing. I'm just a bit rundown. Nothing a whole night's sleep wouldn't put right.' The young woman looked tired, as well she might with three children under five, but she also looked as if she had lost weight recently. Her trousers and blouse looked at least one size too big for her.

But it was as she spoke that alarm bells began to ring in Meagan's head. The woman was having to stop to catch her breath every few words.

'Have a seat, Mrs Munro. Since you're here I may as well take a quick look.'

'It's Rhona,' she replied, giving Meagan a tired smile, reluctantly taking a seat and settling the baby on her lap. 'It's just that I have another two kids at home. A neighbour is looking after them for me, but I need to get back. They can be a bit of a handful.' Rhona smiled ruefully. 'Its no wonder I'm exhausted.'

Meagan lifted the child from Rhona's lap. The little girl protested, reaching chubby arms towards her mother.

'Well, this little one is fine at any rate. Do you mind if Sophie holds her while I have a quick listen to your chest?'

As Meagan listened to Rhona's lungs, her anxiety deepened. There was something wrong.

'Any history of asthma? TB?' she asked.

Rhona shook her head. 'Dr MacDonald thought I might have a chest infection when I came to see him a couple of weeks ago. He put me on antibiotics.'

'And have they helped?' Meagan asked. She looked at the notes Colin had made in his neat hand. He hadn't been totally convinced that Rhona had had a chest infection, but had prescribed a course of antibiotics and asked her to come back and see him in a week. There was no suggestion that Rhona had been back to see him.

'Did you finish the course of antibiotics?' Meagan asked.

Her patient nodded. 'Dr MacDonald was insistent,' she said. 'But they didn't help.'

'I see that he asked you to come back and see him last week,' Meagan said.

'I know. And I meant to come, but I couldn't find the time. The kids keep me so busy.'

After talking a thorough history and giving her another examination Meagan was beginning to suspect she knew what was wrong with her patient and she didn't like it one bit.

She turned to Sophie, who had managed to placate the baby. 'Sophie, would you mind seeing if Dr Stuart is back? If he is, could you ask him to come in for a minute?'

'What is it?' Rhona was beginning to look

anxious. 'Why do you need Dr Stuart? I told you, a day or two's rest, although how I am going to manage that is beyond me—is all I need. I don't want you to go to any more trouble. I've taken up enough of your time as it is.'

Meagan was disappointed when Sophie returned without Cameron. Although she was pretty sure her diagnosis was correct, she wanted another opinion. And if she was right, she needed to arrange further tests.

'Dr Stuart is still at the hospital. I've got him on the line, though,' Sophie told Meagan.

Meagan excused herself to Rhona and went into Cameron's room to take the call.

'Hello, Meagan,' he said without preamble. 'You have a problem?'

Meagan quickly outlined her findings and then, with a slight hesitation, her fears.

'I think she may have a tumour, Cameron. And she's only 26—my age—with three young children.' There. It was out. She had said it.

'You could be right,' Cameron said, his voice soft. 'But there's no point in imagining the worst until we know more. Send her along here for a chest X-ray. Ask her to come straight to the hospital and I can have a look at her before my visits this afternoon.'

'Thank you. The sooner we know what's going on, the better. I'll come too. I'd like to see the X-ray.'

'It's your afternoon off. Why don't you go home and I'll call you once I've had a look at the film?'

Meagan shook her head before realizing he couldn't see her.

'If it's all the same to you, I'd rather come to the hospital,' she said, praying she wouldn't have to argue with him. Rhona was her patient now.

'Of course. I'd do the same in your shoes. I'll see you shortly.'

Meagan hung up and went back to her patient. She explained about the X-ray.

'Are you sure it can't wait? You're not worried about me, are you?' Rhona managed a shaky laugh.

'It could wait, but Dr Stuart is there now, so I see no reason for us to delay. Have you got your car? I could give you a lift, if you like.' Rhona seemed to realise that Meagan was determined to get her to the hospital, and gave in with a weary smile.

'Its OK, I'll take mine. It has the baby seat. I'll just phone my babysitter and let her know I'll be late. You don't think it will take too long, do you?'

As Meagan drove to the hospital she tried to swallow her anxiety. If she was right, what would the diagnosis mean to Rhona and her young family? It was the worst side of medicine, and the bit about general practice Meagan was beginning to realise she'd find the toughest— knowing the people you were about to deliver bad news to. She was already beginning to think of her patients as an extended family.

When she arrived at the hospital, she found Cameron in the emergency reception area, his dark head bent over patients' notes. She watched him for a second. Strangely, she felt comforted knowing he was here and would be helping her look after her patient.

He looked up and, seeing her, stood and crossed the space between them. He brushed her shoulder with a hand as if he knew instinctively that she needed some reassurance.

'Rhona's arrived and is having her X-ray. She won't be long, then we can have a look. But you do know there are a number of things it could be?'

Meagan took a deep breath and returned his look steadily. She didn't want him to think she was the type of doctor who couldn't remain professional at all times.

'I know. But I did take a full history. And it's not that I'm being over-cautious because of Robert Maclean.' She couldn't help but slide a glance in his direction.

'You're just being thorough. That's good. But let's just wait and see. Take it step by step.' Cameron smiled down at her. 'Shall we go and see if they are finished?'

Ten minutes later Cameron had Rhona's X-ray up and Meagan's heart sank. All over the chest were large white circles, indicative of tumours. She looked at Cameron, shocked. He was frowning, his mouth set in a grim line.

'Looks like you were right. It seems pretty clear she has metastasis in her chest,' he said. But Meagan felt no satisfaction at his words. She wished desperately that she had been wrong.

'We need to talk to her,' Cameron said.

'I need to tell her,' Meagan said quietly. 'She's my patient. Although how I'm going to tell a young woman with three small children that it looks as if she has a terminal illness is beyond me.'

Cameron looked thoughtful. 'We'll talk to her together. I've known Rhona for years. I delivered her last two babies. I wonder what the primary source of the tumours are? I'd like to examine her again.'

'Why? What are you thinking?'

'It's a long shot, but you said she'd been nauseous. Has she missed a period?'

'She said she's not had a period since the birth of her baby. She's been breastfeeding, so it's understandable that she hasn't, isn't it? Are you thinking that she's had a tumour through her last pregnancy and that the pregnancy accelerated its growth?'

'No,' Cameron said. 'She was sterilised when she had her last baby. They did it at the time of her C-section. It's something else. See these tumours—the size of them? They are referred to as cannonball tumours.'

Meagan was puzzled. She didn't know where Cameron was going with his thinking.

'I'm going to examine her. I'll ask one of the nursing staff to do a pregnancy test.'

Meagan confusion deepened. Hadn't he just said himself that Rhona couldn't be pregnant? And what was the point in delaying talking to their patient? The sooner they spoke to her, the sooner she they could arrange for her to start treatment. It probably wouldn't give her much more time, but every minute longer she had with her young children would be precious. She felt her throat close and she blinked away tears. However upset she felt, she didn't want Cameron to see it. But it seemed she couldn't hide her feelings quickly enough.

'Hey,' he said, 'let's not get ahead of ourselves.' For a moment it looked as if he was going to reach out to her, but he let his hands drop to his side.

'But she has three young children. How can any woman cope with the thought of leaving them? Why is life so cruel?'

'We'll do out best for her, Meagan. You picked it up, and at least she has a chance to prepare herself. Let's go and see her and then we'll talk again.'

Rhona was waiting in the consulting room, feeding her baby. The baby was sucking contentedly and the three adults watched as her eyes closed and she fell asleep.

'Well?' Rhona asked as she settled her child in her buggy. 'Can I go?'

'I'm afraid you can't. Not yet at any rate,' Cameron said gently.

'Why? What is it?' She looked at the two doctors. 'What is it?' she said again, her voice rising. 'There's something you're not telling me. C'mon, Cameron Stuart. You've known me for years. You know I like straight talking.' Despite her brave words, Meagan could hear the fear in her voice.

'We found something on your chest X-ray that worries us a little.' Cameron said. 'I want to examine you again, if that's all right? But first do you think you could manage to give us a urine specimen?'

'Sure,' Rhona replied. 'But I think you should tell me what this is about.'

'Urine first,' Cameron said firmly. Once the nurse had taken away the sample for testing, Cameron examined Rhona again while Meagan looked on.

'Any lumps or bumps anywhere? In your breasts?'

'Not that I've noticed.'

'Any chance you could be pregnant?' Cameron asked.

Rhona laughed. 'You know as well as I do that the answer to that is no.'

Meagan was still none the wiser. Where was Cameron going with this? Could Rhona be pregnant? She had heard of cases where women had fallen pregnant even after having their tubes tied. That would make it all even worse. She couldn't have treatment while pregnant. The pregnancy would have to be terminated.

'Any other symptoms apart from the breathlessness?'

'No, except for feeling tired all the time—but I put that down to years of sleepless nights.' She laughed nervously. 'You don't think I could be pregnant, do you? Even if I hadn't been sterilized, it wouldn't be possible.' She blushed furiously. 'You know, with having three small children we haven't…not since—I mean I am just so darned exhausted all the time. It's not as if I don't love my husband. Oh, dear…' She tailed off.

'No, I don't think you're pregnant,' Cameron

said. 'I think there's a chance it's something else, but I won't be sure until I get the result of the urine test. We'll have the results shortly. In the meantime, you can get dressed. I'll be back in to see you in a minute.'

Even more confused, Meagan followed Cameron out of the room. He looked satisfied, even cheerful. Didn't he care that they were about to deliver a death sentence to a woman who had three young children depending on her?

Before she had a chance to question him, the nurse arrived back.

'The pregnancy test is strongly positive,' She told Cameron. 'Good news?'

'You could say that,' Cameron said, smiling.

'How can you possibly think it's good news?' Meagan burst out, unable to contain herself any longer. 'If she decides not to terminate then she'll die more quickly and then there will be four children left without a mother.'

Cameron placed a hand on Meagan's shoulder. Something in his expression stopped her in her tracks.

'Have you ever heard of a condition called choriocarcinoma?' Cameron asked.

Meagan shook her head, although somewhere deep in the recesses of her mind the term sounded familiar.

'Well, it's a type of cancer that originates in the placental tissue after a pregnancy or miscarriage,' Cameron explained. 'As far as Rhona's concerned, it is really good news. The tumours will respond quickly to treatment and there is every chance she will make a complete recovery.'

'Are you sure?' Meagan asked, wanting desperately to believe him. But what if he was wrong?

'I'm positive. We'll need to do further tests, of course, but I have no doubt that is what we are seeing here.'

Meagan felt herself sag with relief. If he was right and she had no reason to doubt him, there was every chance Rhona would be around for many years to come. She grinned at him.

'What made you think of it?'

'When I saw the X-ray and the magnitude of the tumours, it got me thinking. With that kind of invasion Rhona should have been much sicker than she is. Then when I examined her and there was no obvious primary source of the tumours, I began to think of choriocarcinoma. I remember reading about it in one of the medical journals a year or so ago. The positive pregnancy test all but confirms the diagnosis. It's still a serious condition, but thankfully it responds extremely well to chemotherapy.'

'Thank God you thought of it. Imagine if you hadn't. We would have told Rhona she was going to die and put her through torment. She might even have decided not to have treatment, in which case she would have died.' Meagan shivered. 'She's a very lucky woman to have you around. I would have missed it if it hadn't been for you.'

'Don't beat yourself up. You did the right thing by discussing her with me and thinking of the chest X-ray. Someone else might just have given her more antibiotics and sent her home. If you hadn't insisted on investigating further when you did, the condition could have advanced quickly to a point where we would have been too late to help Rhona.'

Meagan shuddered. It had been a close call. Thank God she had decided to investigate further and thank God Cameron had been there to look at the X-ray with her. Otherwise she might be having an entirely different conversation with Rhona right now.

'You did well, as did Sophie, by insisting Rhona see you. That's what general practice is all about. A team effort where everyone pulls together. It seems we made the right decision taking you on after all. Well done. Again.'

When Cameron smiled at Meagan, she felt her stomach flip. She smiled back. She couldn't help but feel pleased at his praise. More than anything else she wanted his respect and approval—as a doctor, of course.

'Let's go and tell her the good news, shall we?' he said.

A few days later, on a Saturday afternoon, as Meagan sat outside her cottage, coffee in hand, marvelling at how the sun lit the sky and turned the sea pewter, she was surprised to see Cameron's battered vehicle making its way up the track. He jumped out and walked towards Meagan with long strides. He was wearing faded jeans that moulded to his thighs and a thick dark sweater. At his side was an excited-looking Ian and a shy Effie.

'Dr Galbraith.' Ian ran up to Meagan. 'We're going out in the boat. And Daddy said I could ask if you'd come. You will come, won't you? You said you would.' The little boy was hopping excitedly from foot to foot. 'We have a flask of orange juice and some scones from Jessie.'

Cameron looked apologetic. 'He's been on at me ever since you told him you like going out in boats. I told him that you'd have other things to do, but I agreed we'd ask you.'

All of a sudden she wanted nothing more than to be out in a boat with the wind in her hair. It was such a beautiful day, with just the right amount of breeze. On the other hand, the children had probably put Cameron in a difficult position. Somehow she doubted that he wanted to spend time with her away from work. And did she want to spend more time than absolutely necessary with him?

'Oh, I'm sure you and your daddy will enjoy it better without me,' Meagan said. 'Besides, you have Effie here for company. How are you, Effie?'

Before the small child had a chance to answer Ian interrupted.

'Daddy says we need two adults if Effie is coming too. And she wants to come, don't you, Effie? And Mummy won't come. She says she can't bear boats.' Meagan almost laughed out loud. He had mimicked his mother's voice perfectly. 'Please, Dr Galbraith, say yes.'

Meagan looked at Cameron. She was sure this hadn't been his idea.

'I think Dr Galbraith has other plans, children,' Cameron said softly. 'We can go another time. Why don't we go to the beach instead? We can look for starfish in the rock pools.' He turned to Meagan.

'I'm sorry for the interruption. We'll be on our way. Come on, guys—back into the Jeep.'

But one look at the two small disappointed faces was enough for Meagan to make up her mind. Then she remembered. Even if she wanted to go she couldn't, it was her turn to be on call.

'I'd love to go with you and Effie,' she said a little wistfully, 'but I'm afraid I'm supposed to stay here in case any one gets sick and needs a doctor.'

'If that's all that's stopping you,' Cameron said, 'I've already arranged cover.' He looked a little sheepish. 'One of the GPs in the other practice phoned earlier, asking if they could do this weekend in return for us doing another weekend for them. One of the practice staff is getting married in Inverness in a couple of weeks and they all want to go. They had arranged a locum, but that fell through so they're kind of stuck. I hope that's OK with you? I'm happy to do it if you're not.'

'No, no, don't worry. I'm happy to swap. Any weekend is fine with me. I don't have any plans.'

'Anyway, I thought that this would be a good opportunity for me to take you out and show you where the safe channels are. It means you can go out on your own next time.'

That was the clincher for Meagan. She knew Cameron would never let her use Colin's boat until he was satisfied that she knew where the dangers were.

'In that case,' she said, 'I'd love to come. You need to give me a minute or two to get ready, though. I'll be as quick as I can.

Ian ran around in circles, clearly delighted. Meagan laughed. 'He's a bundle of energy, isn't he?'

She left Cameron and the two children outside while she changed into jeans and a thick jumper. Although it was a beautiful day, she knew once they got out on the water, it would get much cooler. In a small backpack, she packed some waterproofs and a flask of coffee. She hesitated for a moment before picking up a woolly hat she had found lying around. She added it to her bag, along with a picnic blanket. After slipping on some plimsoles, she was ready.

By the time she walked down to the bay below the house, Cameron and his two small helpers had already rigged the boat.

'We'll go out under the engine and put the sails up once we are clear of the bay,' Cameron said. 'It's pretty rocky just here and I need more manoeuvrability than the sails allow. I'll be helmsman, if you'll crew?'

That agreed, and with all of them wearing life-jackets, Meagan cast off and they were on their way. Cameron handled the boat easily, smoothly navigating their way into the open sea. Meagan watched him as he concentrated. At the tiller, he seemed more relaxed than she had ever seen him.

It was as if he was in his element. The wind ruffled his almost too long dark hair.

Once they were out at sea, Meagan and Cameron unfurled the sails. They worked easily together, almost as if they had sailed in partnership for years. Soon they were speeding along. Meagan was thrilled to be back out on the sea. Until now she hadn't realised how much she had missed being on the water.

'Where are we heading?' she yelled across to Cameron.

'If you are up to a bit of hillwalking, I thought we'd take her to the foot of Eaval.' He indicated a hill in the distance. 'It's the highest hill on Uist, although it's a baby compared to most in Scotland. It's an easy climb, even for the children. I thought we could picnic at the top— the views are great there—before coming back down. Is that OK?'

'I'm sure if it's manageable for the children it'll be OK for me.' Meagan grinned back at him. 'Is this as fast as this boat can go?' she challenged.

'It's as fast as I'm prepared to take it with children on board,' Cameron said. 'Perhaps after we drop them off later we can go out again. Then you can show me what you can do.'

Meagan accepted the challenge with a grin. Cameron Stuart had no idea just what she could do with a boat. She was looking forward to showing him. She hoped it would wipe that confident grin off his face.

Before long they were coming into a sheltered bay. Once again they lowered the sails and came in under the engine. Out of the wind, Meagan could feel the heat of the sun on her shoulders. She removed her sweater and tied it around her waist. Cameron indicated for her to hold the tiller then, as they came in, he leapt off the boat onto nearby rocks and tied the boat securely.

'The tide will be on its way out by the time we come back down. 'We'll be able to wade out then. In the meantime, could you pass the children across?'

'I can jump!' Ian protested. 'I'm too old to be lifted—by a girl,' he added, giving Meagan a look of disdain.

'You'll do as you are told, young man,' Cameron said severely. 'Remember what I said. When you are out on a boat you always do exactly what the skipper says. Without argument.'

Something in his father's voice must have told Ian that there was no point in arguing. After Meagan had passed Effie across, Ian allowed Meagan to help him on to the rocks and into his father's arms.

'Wait for us up the hill a bit,' Cameron said, holding his hand out to Meagan. She grabbed her rucksack and took hold of his hand. She felt his roughened hand take hers and she leapt lightly onto the rocks beside him. For the briefest moment he held her to him. She could feel the rough texture of his sweater on her bare arms and the heat of his body on hers. She looked up to find his eyes on hers. They held for a moment then he stood back to let her past.

They walked up the hill at an easy pace, letting the children run on ahead. Cameron insisted on carrying her rucksack as well as his. Soon he stopped and removed his sweater. His T-shirt rode up with the movement and Meagan caught a brief glimpse of his tanned muscular abdomen. Unbidden memories of trailing her hands across the hard muscle of his chest came rushing back.

She felt her ears go pink at the tips. He looked at her and a small smile tugged at the corners of his mouth.

'Work out, do you?' he said, his eyes appraising her.

'I like to keep fit,' she said. 'We can hardly tell our patients to take more exercise and then slob out ourselves, can we?'

However, as they climbed higher Meagan wondered if she would have to eat her words. In order to keep the children in sight Cameron lengthened his stride and it was all Meagan could do to keep up. She was glad he didn't seem in the mood to chat, as she would have found it impossible to talk and walk at the same time.

She was very glad, therefore, when they reached the top of the hill. Meagan had to admit the climb had been worth it. As Cameron had said, the hill wasn't particularly high but they could see for miles under the cloudless sky. Cameron pointed out the neighbouring islands of Skye and Harris.

'If you like hillwalking, you'll enjoy Skye,' he told her. 'If you prefer beaches, then Uist is just a short ferry ride away. You should visit both on your weekends off.'

'I might just do that,' Meagan said. 'Actually, if you think Colin wouldn't mind, I would love to sail his boat across to Uist.'

Cameron frowned. 'Please, Meagan, don't underestimate the conditions around here. Although it's a beautiful day today, the weather can change in a moment. We are always having to rescue unwary tourists from the mountains and the sea. I don't want to have to rescue you. We need you…' He looked into her eyes. Meagan felt her heart thud. What did he mean? Was he implying…?

'The practice needs you,' he finished abruptly. 'Hey, children,' he called out, 'are you ready for something to eat?'

Meagan could have kicked herself. Why was she always reading more into Cameron's behaviour than she should? Hadn't he made it clear enough that their relationship was purely that of two professionals? And the only reason he had invited her on this trip was for the sake of the children.

Shortly after they had finished their picnic,

Cameron stood up. He scanned the sky with practised eyes.

'There are clouds rolling in from the north. Could be there's a storm on the way. We'd better get back. Besides, we can't let the tide get too far out or we'll be stuck here until it comes back in.'

Looking at the sky, Meagan could see no evidence of a storm, although the wind had picked up a bit. Perhaps he'd had enough of her company?

'Fine by me,' she said, gathering their belongings together. The children seemed happy enough to be returning to the boat.

As Cameron had predicted, the tide was on the way out, dragging the boat with it away from the shore. Now there was an expanse of sand to be crossed before they could get to the vessel. She'd have to roll up her jeans and wade out. Cameron had obviously come to the same conclusion. He had already rolled up his jeans, revealing muscular calves, and had removed his shoes.

'It's too deep for you to wade. You'll get soaked. I'll carry you and the children out.'

'No.' Meagan said hastily. It was just too embarrassing. 'I don't mind getting a little wet. I'll soon get dry.'

'Don't be silly,' Cameron said, striding towards her purposefully. Before she had a chance to protest, he had scooped her in his arms and was carrying her out towards the boat. 'Stay there Ian, Effie,' he called over his shoulder. 'Don't move an inch until I come back for you.'

'Put me down,' Meagan snarled at Cameron, struggling in his arms.

'The devil take me,' he said, grinning down at her. 'Why can't you just do as you're told? Anyway, if I let you wade out, the children will want to do the same. Far better all crew get treated the same.'

By this time they were halfway out to the boat and the sea was already above Cameron's knees. Despite her indignation, Meagan was once more acutely aware of his muscular chest and powerful arms as they held her. Her face was inches away from his and she could smell the faint scent of his aftershave. She closed her eyes. She couldn't help it. She fancied him like mad. The thought brought her to her senses. She wriggled in his arms.

'I *said* let me down.' The next second she had her wish. Without a word he dropped her. She slid into the water and, catching her foot on some seaweed, slipped under. She gasped as she was submerged in the icy water. Well, it was one way to cool her libido which after a couple of years without sex seemed to have traitorously gone into overdrive.

The next second she felt her T-shirt being grabbed and she was pulled unceremoniously upwards. She came out of the water, choking and gasping, and looked straight into glinting brown eyes. Without a word Cameron hauled her the last two remaining feet towards the boat and, gripping her under the arms, lifted her onto the side of the boat where she hung like a landed fish, gasping and spluttering. Then she felt him grab her hips as he tossed her all the way over the side onto the deck.

She raised herself to her knees, aware that her hair was plastered to her head. And wasn't that a bit of seaweed she could feel curling around her ear? Any feelings of lust had vanished.

'Do you mind?' she snarled. 'I'm not a salmon or some other fish to be landed. I told you I was perfectly able to get myself on board. And you…' She almost spat out the words, aware that she had worked herself into a fury, but by now unable to stop herself. 'What century do you think we are living in?'

But it was too late. Cameron was already making his way to shore and was out of earshot. As Meagan continued cursing under her breath, he placed Ian onto his back and Effie under his arm and started making his way back.

Although Meagan had managed to regain some of her composure, she wasn't finished with him yet. As he deposited his charges and leapt on board, she muttered at him, 'Just you wait, Cameron Stuart. I'll get my revenge. Just you wait and see.'

'You told me to let you go,' he said easily as he turned the boat in the direction of home. 'I was only doing what I was told. Isn't that what you women want?'

He could hardly admit the truth, he told himself ruefully. That the feel of her in his arms had almost made him lose control. The only way he'd been able to resist the temptation of bringing his lips down on hers had been to dump her unceremoniously into the sea. Hardly a gallant gesture, he acknowledged wryly.

'I'm soaked,' she said through gritted teeth,

removing another piece of seaweed from her hair and looking at it with distaste before throwing it back in the sea.

'Here,' he said rummaging around in the rucksack. 'Get below and change into this. At least you'll be warmer.'

Effie and Ian were trying unsuccessfully to smother their giggles behind their hands. Meagan thought for a moment how she must look and then burst out laughing. Relieved, the children joined her, Ian rolling around the deck hugging his sides. Soon they were all laughing.

Meagan picked up the sweater. 'I'll go get changed, then, shall I? But, Dr Stuart, I meant every word I said. You'll pay for this.'

'There a small gas stove down below,' he said. 'Why don't you make some tea once you've changed?' he suggested.

Below Meagan found a small galley and a couple of berths. She also found a towel which she used to dry her hair as best she could. She slipped out of her wet clothes, leaving her panties on, and pulled Cameron's sweater over her head, catching a faint whiff of his aftershave as she did so. It came to just above her knees.

Well, sweater dresses were all the rage, she thought ruefully, although she was pretty certain the catwalk didn't have a version like the one she was wearing. She was equally certain that the catwalk didn't have models whose hair hung in rats' tails either. Needless to say, she hadn't thought to bring her comb with her. Then she remembered the woolly hat. It would cover the worst of the damage, she thought, pulling it over her head and tucking her damp hair inside. Still plotting her revenge, she set about making some tea.

When Meagan appeared from below deck, Cameron almost dropped the tiller. Even with her face devoid of make-up and her hair hidden under the ridiculous hat, she was as beautiful as any woman Cameron had ever seen. Without the distraction of her hair, her perfect cheekbones, wide mouth and striking green eyes stood out. Beneath his sweater her legs seemed to go on for ever. Barefoot, she oozed sensuality and he felt heat in his belly. But he had to keep his distance from her, no matter how difficult it was. The last thing he or Meagan needed was island gossip.

And if talk got back to Rachel, or if Rachel even suspected he had feelings for Meagan, he had no doubt that she would carry out her threat and sue for custody of their son. And with the hours he worked, she stood every chance of winning. She wouldn't do it, not as long as she thought there was a chance, however remote, of them getting back together. Despite the feelings he had for Meagan, and they had never truly gone away, he would never risk losing his son. But, he thought, glancing over once more at Meagan, it was going to be a lot harder keeping his hands off this woman than he had ever thought possible. He almost groaned aloud.

'Nice hat,' he said instead.

CHAPTER FIVE

BY THE time they arrived back at the bay in front of Meagan's house the wind had picked up. Dark clouds were scudding across the sky and the first drops of rain were starting to fall. It seemed as though Cameron's weather predictions had been right, and he hadn't been making excuses to cut their trip short after all. As Meagan tidied the boat in preparation for leaving, she knew the worsening weather meant there was little chance she and Cameron would be heading out again later. Probably a good thing—although she longed to give him a taste of his own medicine. Already a plan for revenge was forming in her mind.

As she stood forward of the boat, ready to leap out with the ropes to fasten her, she noticed a slim, blonde figure watching them approach. Rachel! She had probably come down to collect the children and take them home, Meagan thought. Or perhaps she was checking up on Cameron. With a shock of dismay, Meagan realised she was still dressed in very little except Cameron's jumper. It was too late to do anything about it now. And anyway, whatever Rachel thought, whatever was between Cameron and his ex-wife, it had nothing to do with her.

Ian ran towards his mother as soon as he got ashore. 'Mummy,' he said, 'you'll never guess. Dr Galbraith jumped in the water. Daddy said she fancied a swim. But then she was all wet and had to put on Daddy's clothes. And she had seaweed in her hair and she looked cross. Then we all laughed and she did too. We had such a good time. I wish you would have come with us.'

'You know I don't like getting wet, darling,' Rachel said, her cool eyes regarding Meagan disdainfully. Meagan felt self-conscious and embarrassed standing before this immaculate woman and wearing Cameron's clothes.

'I thought I'd come and check that you are having dinner with us at the House, Cameron. I have to go back to London tomorrow for a few days, but I'll be back in time for the ball.'

Ian looked at his mother. His lower lip trembled.

'You don't have to go back already, Mummy. You said you were staying for ages this time. Daddy, tell Mummy she can't go. She has to stay here with us.'

Cameron's eyes were hooded. He looked at his ex-wife.

'Do you have to go? Can't you stay a little longer? For your son's sake, if nothing else?'

'You know I can only tolerate it here for so long, Cameron. Besides, I need a new dress for the dance as well as checking in with the agency. I'll be back before you know it.' She reached out and tweaked her son's cheek. 'You know I'd take you with me if I could, don't you, darling? But there's school. And anyway Daddy doesn't like me to take you away.' She slid a look in Cameron's direction, seemingly waiting for a response. When she didn't get one she continued, 'I think we'd better leave Dr Galbraith to get dressed, don't you, Cameron?' She raised an elegant eyebrow in Meagan's direction. 'I'd invite you to dinner, but I'm sure you have plenty you'd rather be getting on with. My family has taken up too much of your time as it is.'

Meagan felt herself flush under the woman's

thinly veiled hostility. She couldn't imagine wanting to spend an evening in her company.

'No, I think I'll have a long bath and watch a movie. Thanks all the same.' Meagan turned to Ian and Effie.

'Thank you both very much for your company this afternoon. I can't remember when I last had such good crew.'

'Does that mean we can do it again?' Ian's cheerful smile had disappeared. Once again he looked like the solemn child older than his years that Meagan had first met.

'Any time. You just phone me whenever it's a good day, and if I'm free we'll just pack a picnic and go. If that's all right with you?' Meagan asked Rachel.

'Whatever,' Rachel replied, shrugging her shoulders and looking bored. 'Although I have to say I'm surprised, if you are so keen on kids, that you haven't any of your own.'

Meagan flinched. Was it possible that this woman knew? No, it couldn't be. No one knew except Charlie. It had been a stab in the dark. Rachel couldn't know. She picked up her rucksack and shivering, through whether it was from the cold or something else she couldn't be sure.

'I'll return your sweater to the surgery, Cameron. Now, if you'll excuse me, I'll say good-night.' She walked away and didn't look back.

Later that evening the weather turned stormy. The rain was lashing against the windows and they rattled at the onslaught. Meagan was surprised at how quickly the weather had changed, just as Cameron had predicted. He had been right to cut their boat trip short.

Meagan shivered. The house felt cool and she eyed the fire apprehensively before rolling up her sleeves and making an attempt at getting it going. Happily, after her third failed attempt Mrs McLeod appeared, and with a certain amount of disdainful clucking got it going for her.

'I'll do it for you this time, but watch carefully so you can manage yourself next time. I won't always be around to help.'

Meagan was getting the distinct impression that the housekeeper didn't approve of her.

'I'm sure I'll manage next time. I'm quite good at picking things up.'

Mrs McLeod harrumphed, lifted the pail by the fire and headed towards the door.

'Where are you going with the bucket?' Meagan asked.

'Out to the peat stack at the back of the house. You'll need more to see the fire through the evening.'

'Oh, no, you don't. It's wild out there.' Meagan took the pail from the protesting woman's fingers. 'If anyone's going, its me.'

Reluctantly, Mrs McLeod let Meagan take the bucket. She handed her a torch. 'Here. You'll need this. It's as black as the peat you're going for out there.'

By the time Meagan returned, Mrs. McLeod had set a pot of tea and a couple of scones on the table, and was tying a scarf around her head.

'Get out of those wet things and warm yourself by the fire,' she said brusquely, but Meagan could tell that she was beginning to unbend. 'I'll be off to the house before the weather gets any worse.'

Immediately, Meagan put her jacket back on. 'I'll run you up quickly.'

'No, indeed you won't,' the older woman protested. 'We island women are a lot tougher than you city girls. Although—' she smiled at Meagan '—you are not quite as useless as I thought you might be.'

Before Meagan had a chance to protest further, Mrs. McLeod had left.

Once she'd had a bath and something to eat Meagan, took her book and curled up in front of the fire. The wind had risen further and the little house shook as the wind rattled the windows. She was glad that she didn't have to be out on a night like this. Once or twice the lights flickered. She had been warned that the electricity often went down during storms. Meagan hoped there were some candles stashed somewhere, but if not she'd just have to make do with an early night. Not a bad idea, she thought as she toasted her feet in the warmth of the fire and snuggled deeper into her thick dressing-gown.

She was just about to go to bed when there was a knock at the door. As she opened it, the force of the wind almost took it out of her hand. Standing in front of her was Cameron. His hair was plastered to his forehead and he was dressed in oilskins.

'Can I come in?' He had to shout to make himself heard above the wind. It would serve him right if I left him there, Meagan thought. Then he'd know what it felt like to be soaked to the skin. But something in Cameron's expression told her that this was no social call. Silently she stood back and let him enter. He strode over to the fire and warmed his hands.

'We need your help, Meagan,' he said. 'One of the fishing boats didn't return this evening. Search and Rescue are sending a helicopter. It's too stormy for a lifeboat. I'm going with them but we need all hands on deck at the hospital if we find them. And that means all the doctors at both practices. There are four men on that boat.' He looked anguished. 'And I know them all.'

'Of course. I'll get dressed straight away. But why didn't you phone? I could have gone straight to the hospital.'

'Have you tried your phone in the last couple of hours?' he asked. 'The lines are down. The mobiles too. It doesn't help with the communication problems. And, anyway, I didn't want you driving to the hospital on your own. It's high tide later tonight and the wind is already pushing the waves over the causeways. If you don't know exactly where you are going it's easy to lose your way. But we will need both cars, so you'll have to follow me closely. I hope to God people have stayed off the road.'

As Meagan ran upstairs to get dressed he called after her, 'Be as quick as you can, Meagan. I need to be ready to leave the minute the chopper gets here.'

Within minutes they were making their slow way towards the hospital. Meagan was gripping the steering-wheel so tightly she could feel her nails digging into the palms of her hands. Even with the wipers on their fastest setting she could barely see the road in front of her. Instead, she concentrated on following the red rear lights of Cameron's Jeep. As they crossed the causeway that separated the two islands, water spewed over her four-wheel-drive. For one horrifying moment Meagan thought she was going to be swept away. Why had she ever thought life was going to be unexciting here?

At last they arrived at the hospital, only to find that they were the only medics there so far. The doctors who lived on the south of the island were still making their way. However Meagan was relieved to find that Dorothy and Sophie from the practice had managed it and were waiting with the three hospital nurses to offer what help they could.

'Any sign of the helicopter yet?' Cameron asked.

'They haven't been able to take off yet. They're waiting for another crew member and for the wind to die down.'

Cameron cursed. 'The longer those men are out there, the less chance they have.'

'Cameron, I've got the coastguard on the radio.' Dorothy handed Cameron the radio receiver. 'Luckily we have radio contact still,' she said to Meagan. 'The hospital here is well set up, thank goodness, for emergencies like these.'

Everyone listened in silence as Cameron took the call. It was evident from his expression that it was more bad news. As he replaced the receiver he turned to the anxious group, his expression grim.

'More trouble, I'm afraid. A car has gone over the side of one of the causeways. Luckily it isn't submerged—at least not yet—but the driver is trapped and the tide is rising. The fire brigade is on it's way now. Dorothy, could you get me the surgical kit? I need to go. The driver may have to be cut out.'

'I'll go, Cameron,' Meagan offered quietly. 'You wait here for the helicopter.'

He shook his head. 'It'll be at least an hour before it's here. The other doctors should be here by then if I'm not back.'

'Then I'm coming with you,' Meagan said. 'No argument. We can keep in touch with the hospital by radio. If the helicopter looks as if it's on its way and the others haven't made it by then, one of us can come back.'

'I haven't time to argue. Dorothy, we'll take the radio with us. Keep in touch. Come on, then, Meagan. Let's go. We'll take my car. It's too risky for you on your own.'

Once again Meagan had to brave the lashing rain and wind. She couldn't begin to imagine what it was like for the fishermen. If they were alive they must be freezing as well as shocked. Although the outside air temperature wasn't particularly cold, she knew the temperature of the Atlantic sea could kill within minutes.

It took them ten minutes to drive to the causeway connecting the middle Island to the southern one. The fire engine was there before them and they were glad of its flashing lights to guide them quickly and safely towards the stricken vehicle. Cameron was out of the car almost before he had brought it to a halt and Meagan hurried after him.

'Any luck, Angus?' he called out to the fireman as he approached.

'Hello, Cameron, it's good to see you,' the burly islander responded. 'It's a visitor to the island. His wife and two kids were in the car with him. We've managed to get everyone but the driver out. His foot is stuck and the tide is rising. It's up to his shoulders now and he's beginning to panic.'

'Any chance you could pull the car out, occupant and all?' Cameron asked.

'We've already thought of that. But I'm afraid there's no chance. If we had more time then maybe. As it is, we have ten, maybe fifteen minutes left before the water rises above his neck level.'

'Right, then, let's take a look.' Cameron slid down the side of the causeway and slipped into the water. Tall though he was, the water came up to his hips. The front of the car was pointing downwards, meaning that the driver would be even lower than they were. Meagan knew that unless Cameron could release the man, they would have to amputate the foot. But she didn't know if it was even possible to amputate below water. And if they couldn't amputate, what would they do? They couldn't just leave him to drown.

She slid down the slope after Cameron, knowing that a fireman was following with the medical kit held above his head clear of the swirling water. Whatever Cameron decided to do, he'd need help. She watched as, after leaning through the passenger window to say a few words to the frightened but conscious driver, Cameron's head dropped below the water. A minute later he surfaced.

'It's pretty murky down there,' he shouted over the wind. 'Even if I had time to amputate, there is no way I'd be able to see well enough. However, there is a little bit of space between his foot and the pedal. I think I might be able to pull it out with brute force. I am just going down for another look. Keep an eye on the patient, would you?'

As he dropped once more below the surface of the water, Meagan slid into the freezing cold water, gasping as she felt herself lose feeling. If it was this cold for her and she was only in up to her waist, what would it be like for the car driver? She also knew that the car was in a precarious position. At any moment it could slide deeper into the water, taking its occupant—and possibly Cameron—with it. She realised they were working against the clock.

'What's your name, sir?' she asked

'Richard,' he said.

He looked pale and his lips were blue. With the cold, or did he have internal injuries? Whatever the reason, Meagan was sure he was going into shock soon, if he didn't drown first. She reached into the bag for an oxygen mask and cylinder. 'Could you hold on to the cylinder?' she asked the fireman standing beside her. She slipped the mask over Richard's face, talking to him in a calm voice. 'We'll give you something for the pain in a second,' she said.

Suddenly the car, with a screeching of metal on rock, started to slide further into the sea. The fireman pulled Meagan away from the car, preventing her from being dragged with it.

Meagan held her breath as for one dreadful moment she thought the car was going to completely disappear under the water, but it stopped after sliding a few inches. Without thinking about the danger, Meagan went back down after it. Richard grasped for her hand and held it. He was clearly terrified. Meagan looked around for Cameron. Had he been trapped under the moving car? She couldn't stop herself crying out with relief when his head reappeared.

'Whew! That was close,' he said, and unbelievably he winked at Meagan. Was it possible that the man was actually enjoying the danger?

'I think we can get him out if the firemen pull while I manoeuvre his ankle. The only thing, Richard,' he said, turning to the patient, 'is I'm almost sure your ankle is broken. It's going to be pretty painful doing it this way.'

Richard lowered his mask and managed a nervous smile. 'A bit of pain is better than the alternative, wouldn't you say?' he said. 'Just do what ever you have to, but get me out of here.'

The wind was still rising and the waves

whipped the words from his mouth, but Meagan knew what Cameron intended to do.

'There's no time, Meagan. We have to give him a shot of morphine, then the firemen will pull him out while I dislodge his ankle. It'll be painful, but with a bit of luck he'll pass out.'

In the end it happened just as Cameron said it would. They got him out and he came around in the ambulance a few minutes later.

'My family?' he moaned. 'Are they all right?'

'Yes. They've gone ahead to the hospital to be checked over,' Meagan soothed the frantic man.

Richard tried to sit up.

'Just relax. It's only a precaution. They're fine. They didn't leave until they knew you were safely out of the car and we promised we were right behind them.'

He sank back down and Meagan replaced the oxygen mask.

'You go in the ambulance with him. I'll drive,' Cameron said.

Meagan looked at Cameron. His hair was plastered to his forehead and streams of water ran down his face. Although he must be very cold, he showed no signs of discomfort. If anything,

Meagan thought he looked entirely at home with the elements. She, on the other hand, was shivering.

Cameron ran to his Jeep and returned with a thick jacket.

'Here,' he said. 'Put this around you. When you get to the hospital, make sure you get out of those wet clothes immediately.'

'Second time today I've been soaked,' Meagan said, attempting a smile. 'And the second time today I've borrowed your clothes.'

Cameron looked at her. 'You did all right back there.' He grinned and Meagan's heart thudded. But before she could reply he was running back to his car.

The hospital was a hive of activity when Meagan arrived with Richard in the ambulance. The injured man's family were sitting in blankets, looking bedraggled and shocked, but according to Dorothy they were fine except for a few cuts and bruises. Not having taken the time to change out of his wet clothes, Cameron was on the radio.

'The helicopter still can't take off,' he said. 'They'll let us know as soon as they can. But another trawler has spotted the boat. It's still afloat, although limping slightly. It's too choppy for the trawler to get any closer, but there's still hope that the men are all right. In the meantime, I'm afraid there is nothing we can do except wait.'

'Hey, Cameron, will you, please, go and get changed?' Dorothy said crossly. 'You're dripping all over the floor.' Despite her tone, Meagan could see she was simply concerned about him. 'Richard's ankle is being X-rayed and then if, as we suspect it is broken, we'll attend to it. He'll need to stay the night. In fact, the whole family should. There's no way they can go back out in this.'

Cameron stood for a moment surveying his team. Satisfied that everything was under control, his eyes lighted on Meagan.

'Dr Galbraith, did I not give strict orders that you were to change out of those clothes the minute you got back?'

'I think you should use the shower first,' Meagan said. 'I'll stay with the patients.'

With a couple of strides Cameron was by her side. 'Out of here,' he growled. 'Unless you want me to lift you bodily into the shower?'

Aware of the amused glances from the staff and certain that Cameron would do what he threatened, Meagan backed out hastily. 'I'll only be a minute,' she said.

When she returned, wearing a clean pair of scrubs and some theatre clogs she had found in the changing room, Dorothy thrust a steaming cup of coffee into her hands. Suddenly she felt exhausted. It had been a long day and it wasn't over yet. She couldn't remember the last time she'd had so much physical exercise. Who needed a gym? She put the cup down and closed her eyes, letting the warmth of the department seep into her bones.

She must have fallen asleep briefly, because the next thing she knew she was being lifted onto a gurney and covered by a blanket. She looked up through half-closed eyes to find Cameron looking down at her, his expression inscrutable. She started to sit up, but he pressed her back down.

'Take a rest while you can,' he said. As she started to protest he stopped her words with a finger on her lips. 'It's good to rest when you can. I promise I'll let you know when we need you.'

When she next woke up, the wind seemed to have died down a bit, and the rain only lashed against the windows sporadically. Cameron had also changed into scrubs and was just replacing the radio handset.

'The coastguard is taking off. They'll be with us in about twenty minutes,' he said. 'They are going to pick me up so I can go with them. They've re-established contact with the fishing boat and it seems that one of the crew has a suspected head injury. They are going to winch me down so I can make an assessment.'

How could he look so calm? Meagan thought. But his brow was furrowed and lines of tiredness were evident around his eyes.

'I can go instead of you,' Meagan offered. 'I've had a rest so I'm probably fitter.'

Cameron looked at her and grinned, the dimples at the corners of his mouth evident.

'You are a brave woman, Dr Galbraith. And thanks, but no. I'm a volunteer member of the coastguard and I've been trained for this. You haven't. You stay here and wait for our return.'

Meagan could see that while she had been asleep one of the doctors from the other practice had arrived. There were more than enough people to cope at the hospital.

'Let me come on the helicopter at least,' she pleaded. 'I've never been on one before. I promise I won't get in the way.'

Cameron frowned, considering her proposal.

'All right, then, but only if you promise not to get in the way. It's probably not a bad idea to have another doctor ready to assess any casualties. But if there is any chance at all that you'll be frightened, let one of the others go. The last thing any of us need is a scared doctor getting in our way.'

'Don't you know by now, Dr Stuart, that nothing frightens me? At least, nothing physical,' she added under her breath, turning away so he wouldn't catch her words.

The airport where the helicopter would be landing was only a few minutes away by car and had already touched down when Meagan and Cameron arrived.

'This is Dr Galbraith.' Cameron introduced her as a member of the crew helped them on with suits and harnesses. 'She's coming too.'

The crewman nodded. 'Been up before?' he asked Meagan as he made the final adjustments to her harness. Meagan shook her head. 'But I love flying.'

The crewman, who introduced himself as Jamie, smiled and handed her a set of headphones. 'It gets pretty noisy up there. You'll need these. I have to warn you it's going to be a bumpy ride.'

Meagan glanced over at Cameron. He looked perfectly at home in his outfit, as if he had been flying all his life. He searched her eyes as if checking out her anxiety levels before, satisfied, grinning at her and giving her a thumbs-up.

He reached over and made a slight adjustment to her helmet. Meagan felt the warmth of his fingers sweep across her jaw.

'It's going to be rough out there. Last chance to change your mind,' he murmured, his voice low. 'No one will think any the worse of you.'

She held his glance. His eyes were warm and steady. She felt her heart flutter. Maybe she was a little nervous, she thought. Why else would her heart be racing?

'Let's get on with it,' she said, climbing into the helicopter. 'We don't want to keep those poor men waiting any longer than they have to.'

It was as turbulent in the air as Jamie had

warned. Once the helicopter lurched and dropped. Despite herself, Meagan gasped and grabbed Cameron's thigh, momentarily squeezing her eyes closed. When she dared to open them again it was to find Cameron looking down at her, amused.

'Did any one ever tell you that you have strong hands Meagan?' He grinned. Embarrassed, she forced herself to uncurl her fingers and remove her hand. But the sensation of his rock-hard thigh muscles stayed in her fingertips. Now was not the time! She had to concentrate on the job ahead.

'When we locate the vessel, they'll winch me down.' Cameron's voice crackled through her headphones. 'I'll make an assessment, then they'll send down the stretcher. While I'm getting the patient strapped onto the stretcher, they'll lift anyone who doesn't need assistance. Once they are on board, you'll need to carry out another assessment and make sure they receive any treatment they need. Get them warmed up at least. OK?'

'Aye, aye, sir,' Meagan said, getting into the swing of things. 'Or should I say Roger that? Like they do in the movies?'

Cameron rolled his eyes at her, then smiled. Meagan admitted to herself that she loved the way the dimples appeared in his cheeks when he smiled. Then, just as quickly, she berated herself. What was the matter with her? She was behaving like a hormonally charged teenager. It must be the adrenaline.

She was interrupted from her wayward thoughts by the pilot announcing that they had found the missing fishing boat. Meagan peered through the rain but could see nothing except waves stretching as far as the eye could see. Cameron touched her shoulder and pointed slightly forward from where Meagan was looking. Eventually her eyes could just make out the shape of the stricken vessel beneath them. It wasn't a particularly big boat. Probably just big enough for the four man crew and their catch. The fishing boat was listing to the side as if it had taken water on board. On the deck stood three of the fishermen, waving frantically. One was gesticulating at the deck, but apart from that they seemed unharmed. It seemed it was the only the fourth absent fisherman that they would have to worry about.

As the helicopter hovered, Cameron made his final preparations to be winched down.

'I'll send up the three men while I'm checking out the injured man,' he reiterated. Hopefully it won't take too long to get everyone on board.' Then before Meagan had a chance to reply he was being lowered towards the boat.

She watched, her heart in her mouth, as the cable holding Cameron swayed in the wind. Underneath them the fishing vessel was also continuously moving, one minute rising towards them, then the next falling away. Meagan now knew that she had completely underestimated the risk Cameron was—they were all—taking. She knew if it weren't for the skill of the crew the helicopter could crash or, and she shuddered at the thought, Cameron could be crushed against the moving boat. She could barely bring herself to watch until finally Cameron was on the boat and unhooking himself from the winch. 'Thank God,' she prayed under her breath. He'd made it.

But the danger wasn't over yet. They still had to get everyone on board. A few heart-stopping minutes later the first fisherman appeared in the doorway of the chopper. Meagan and Jamie pulled him on board, where he lay gasping and shivering. Meagan had only enough time to satisfy herself that he was cold and shocked but otherwise unharmed before the next fisherman was pulled in.

As she examined the second man, she could feel the first man pulling at the sleeve of her jacket. He leant close, shouting in her ear.

'It's Jock who's hurt. The rest of us are all right. But Jock was hit on the back of his head by the equipment we use to lift the fish. He's in a bad way.'

'Try not to worry.' Meagan had to yell to make herself heard above the roar of the helicopter and the sound of the wind. 'Dr Stuart will look after him.'

'I don't think he can move him,' the man yelled back. 'I think he's hurt his spine. He hasn't been able to move his arms or legs since.'

Meagan, satisfied that the second man was also essentially unhurt, moved on to the last man who by this time had been winched on board. At the same time she was thinking frantically about what she'd been told. What if Jock had sustained injuries to his spine? Could they take the risk of moving him? Even strapped to the stretcher, surely it was too much of a risk? But what else could they do? They couldn't leave him there.

Once again Cameron's voice crackled in her ear, this time confirming her worst fears.

'I'm sorry, guys, but you'll have to leave us here for the time being. I think Jock may have fractured his spine. I don't want to take any chances trying to manoeuvre him onto the stretcher. Even with help it's too much of a risk.'

'Roger that,' came the pilot's reply. 'Is the boat capable of staying afloat until we can get someone to tow you in?'

'It had better be,' came the grim reply, 'otherwise you could say we are truly sunk. I'm going to take off my radio for a couple of minutes so I can listen to Jock's chest. I'll speak to you again when I've finished.'

The last man on board was shouting something at Jamie. Meagan couldn't make out the words but she could tell Jamie was worried.

'What is it?' She asked.

'He says Cameron hurt himself when he landed on the deck of the boat. He took a blow to his forehead.'

'In that case, I'm going down. He'll need help.'

'Sorry, no can do,' Jamie said. 'It's too dangerous for a woman. Besides, Cameron will have my guts for garters if I let you go down. And I'm not having that.'

Meagan pulled herself to her full height.

'In this scenario, don't think of me as a woman,' she said through gritted teeth. 'Think of me as a doctor. And if you don't let me go down, *I'll* have your guts for garters.'

Something in the look she gave him must have convinced him. 'What do you think, Captain?' he asked.

'I don't like it,' came the reply, 'but I don't know what else we can do. He needs help and I need you on board. But if we are going to drop her down, we need to do it now.'

'OK, then, Doctor, let's get you hooked up.'

When Meagan felt herself being lowered from the helicopter she felt truly scared for the first time. The rope swayed with the combined turbulence of the helicopter's blades and the wind. She also knew with certainty that Cameron would be furious when he saw her. At that precise moment she didn't know what she feared most—this awful sensation of being buffeted by the wind or Cameron's anger.

Sure enough, when he reached out to pull her onto the deck he was livid. Meagan could see that he had sustained a nasty gash on his forehead which was bleeding profusely. He seemed oblivious to the rivulets of blood that streamed down his face.

'What on earth are you thinking?' he said. 'I'm going to tell them to winch you right back up.' Before he could act on his threat, Meagan had unhooked herself, just as Jamie had shown her, and was giving the helicopter a thumbs-up.

'The men told me you had hurt your head. You can't look after a patient properly if you're hurt yourself,' Meagan said firmly. 'I want to take a look at it.'

She could see that Cameron wasn't finished with her yet, but there was little he could do as the helicopter had already left.

'Let's get below out of the wind. Jock's there already.'

Meagan watched anxiously as Cameron used the rails at the side of the steps to go below. She wanted to check Cameron's injury, but she knew, for the time being, that keeping the boat afloat was the more urgent issue. It was listing to one side, rising with each wave and still taking on water. She knew she needed to keep the boat turned into the wind as best she could or there would be the danger of the boat taking on more water with every wave and capsizing. Now that she was actually on the boat she felt happier. The sea had never frightened her. Just as long as you treated it with respect and kept your cool.

She made her way to the wheelhouse to turn the stricken boat into the wind. She knew she would have to stay at the wheel until help reached them, hopefully before too long.

An irate Cameron appeared.

'What are you doing here?' he said.

'I'm staying here,' Meagan replied. 'If you need me to help with Jock, that's a different matter, but unless you do, this is where I'll be.'

'Jock's stable for the moment. Why don't I steer the boat and you keep an eye on Jock?'

'Tell me, Cameron, can you do something about the wound on your head?'

Cameron touched his head gingerly. 'It just

needs a dressing—something to keep it from bleeding,' he said.

'It's settled, then,' Meagan said. 'You go back below and sort your head out and keep an eye on Jock. You're the one with more medical experience and I'm the one who knows how to keep a boat afloat. I'm staying here. If I need you, I'll yell—I promise.'

The next two hours passed slowly. Meagan kept the boat headed into the wind, knowing that as long as she did that they should stay afloat. Every now and again Cameron would check to see that she was still all right. The second time he appeared he had bandaged his head—and not made a very good job of it either, Meagan thought perversely. She ignored his entreaties for her to change places with him. After a time the rain and wind began to ease and visibility improved. At last she made out the shape of the lifeboat coming towards them. She used the intercom to let Cameron know and as soon as the lifeboat was secured next to them she went below. Cameron was sitting beside Jock, explaining that soon they'd be moving him. Cameron looked exhausted, and from the lines around his mouth Meagan knew he must be in a great deal of pain.

She dropped to her knees to examine his head. It was, however, impossible to make a reliable assessment without undoing the bandage and that was likely to start the wound bleeding again.

'You should have taken something for the pain,' she said.

He smiled tiredly at her. 'I needed to keep my wits about me. I'll take something later.'

It took less than half an hour for them to get back to dry land. The air ambulance was standing by ready to transfer Jock to the specialist spinal unit in Glasgow, although to every one's relief he was beginning to experience a return of feeling to his limbs. Cameron offered to travel with him, but the doctor from the other practice had already volunteered.

'I'm rested,' he told Cameron. 'Besides, it looks as if you could do with a couple of stitches.'

Cameron reluctantly agreed to let Meagan suture his wound.

'I could do it myself,' he growled. 'Just give me a mirror.'

'Don't be ridiculous,' Meagan said. 'Of course you can't manage yourself. I'll do it.'

'I just hope you're not seeing double with tiredness,' he complained. 'You need to get some sleep.'

But eventually, seeing that Meagan was determined, he let her close the wound. He hardly flinched when she injected some local anaesthesia. As she cleaned the gash, he grabbed her hand. 'You did well out there,' he said. 'You're a very brave woman, but I wish you hadn't put yourself in danger.' His eyes glinted as he held her gaze. Meagan felt her spine tingle.

'Why? Were you worried about me?' she teased.

'You're my responsibility,' he said. 'I promised Colin I would look after you. How would the practice cope if both of us had been lost?'

Meagan felt an irrational stab of disappointment. Was that how he saw her? His responsibility? Was that all? But, of course, she was forgetting about Rachel. No doubt he was still in love with her and hoping for a reconciliation. Meagan dismissed the slice of pain she felt at the thought. He had chosen Rachel over her once before, and would probably do so again. She of all people could never—would never—come between two people if there was even the smallest chance they could patch things up, especially when there was a child involved. She began to stitch, resisting the urge to stab him with her needle.

'It seems to me that you are the one needing to be looked after. You're the one who's hurt after all. There's not a scratch on me.'

He grinned and the tiredness left his features.

'Ah, Meagan, why was our timing all wrong?'

She wasn't sure what he was saying. Did he mean he wished he'd met her before Rachel? And if so how, did she feel about that? Her heart gave another flip. She knew how she felt. She knew deep in her bones that she and Cameron were meant for each other. She had known it the first time she had met him and she knew it now. She could love this man. She could love him with every fibre of her being. But it was too late. Much too late.

By the time Cameron and Meagan left the hospital, the sun was beginning to climb in the sky. The wind had almost dropped completely and it looked as if the day would turn out fine.

Meagan guessed she wouldn't be seeing most of it. A warm bath, something to eat then bed, she promised herself. Then she fell asleep.

She woke to the sensation of being lifted gently out of the car. She knew she should resist, but she felt so comfortable held against Cameron's chest. He kicked her front door open and with her still in his arms climbed the stairs two at a time. She felt herself being lowered onto the bed. She wanted to open her eyes and say something, but they felt too heavy. For once she was unable to resist being taken care of. Besides, she didn't have the energy to fight this man all the time.

Just before she gave in to sleep once more, she felt lips as light as a feather brush her temple. She thought she heard him murmur her name, but when she opened her eyes he had gone.

CHAPTER SIX

MEAGAN slept until lunchtime. After dressing, she checked the phone and was relieved to find the lines had been restored. The nurse at the hospital told her that all the patients from the night before were doing fine and not to worry about coming in as Dr Stuart had already done rounds a few hours earlier and was expected back shortly.

Did the man never sleep? Meagan wondered.

Conceding that there was little point in her going to the hospital, she decided to take a walk up to the big house to see Jessie. It would do her good to stretch her aching legs, she thought. It felt as if every bone in her body had been attacked with a hammer.

Jessie opened the door to her. She seemed delighted to see her. 'Come on in,' she said. 'I'll just put on the kettle and then you can tell me all about last night's excitement. Goodness, Meagan, ever since you arrived, it's been all go.'

Meagan collapsed into a comfy chair and related the night's events, interrupted only by Jessie's oohs and aahs.

'He's something else, our Cameron, isn't he?' Jessie said, giving Meagan a coy look from her lively green eyes.

Meagan realised she must have being going on a bit about Cameron. But anyone who had seen him in action the night before would have told the same tale.

'C'mon, Jessie. You can stop looking at me like that. As I told you before, I'm not looking for a relationship.'

'But,' Jessie said, glancing at Meagan's ringless left hand, 'you're not married. Or have you left someone back home?'

'I was married, Jessie,' Meagan said, surprised that she could say the words without flinching inside, 'but he was killed in a car crash a couple of years ago.'

Jessie reached for Meagan's hand. 'I'm so sorry.' She paused. 'I lost my husband too. He died of a brain aneurysm not long after Effie was born.' She shook her head and offered Meagan a small smile. 'It seems we have more in common than we thought. You think you'll never get over it then one day you wake up and life seems bearable again. It might seem right now as if that'll never happen but it does.'

'At least you had Effie,' Meagan said, trying to keep the envy from her voice.

'Yes. To a large degree, having her to look after is what saw me through those first awful weeks and months. Obviously you and your husband didn't have any.'

Meagan bit her lip. She hardly knew Jessie, but already it felt as if they were good friends. She had never really talked to anyone before about what had happened.

'About twelve months before Charlie died, I discovered I was pregnant. At first I wasn't happy—I thought we were too young and that a baby would ruin my career plans—but after a day or two I got used to the idea. Then, as it became more real to me, I decided to hell with a career, a baby was more important.'

'What happened?'

'I had an ectopic pregnancy. The embryo

lodged in one of my Fallopian tubes. They had to operate and remove my tube. While they were operating, they discovered that the other tube was damaged. It's impossible for me to get pregnant naturally. Odd, huh? Losing the baby made me realise how much I wanted children. Now all that's gone for good.' Her voice cracked slightly. Losing the baby and the chance to have children still hurt.

'Poor you.' Jessie looked into the distance. 'I don't know if I could have borne Hamish's death if I hadn't had Effie,' she said softly, before reaching out and taking Meagan's hand. 'Could you try IVF? A friend of mine got pregnant that way.'

'I don't think it would be for me. Anyway, I have no intention of marrying again, so the question of having children is moot. Do you mind if we talk about something else?'

Jessie looked at her sympathetically, before changing the subject.

'About last night,' she said. 'Weren't you scared at all?'

The question took Meagan by surprise. Probably because she hadn't thought about it.

She supposed she should have been but somehow, working alongside Cameron, she hadn't been scared at all. At least, not for herself. There had been moments when she had been worried about the patients and more than one moment when she had been terrified on Cameron's behalf, as any colleague would have been, but no she hadn't been truly scared.

'That's just it, Jessie—I loved every moment!' she said. 'Instead of being frightened, I was exhilarated. Funny to think that when I came here, it was for a quiet life.'

'In that case, you and Cameron have a lot in common. He's always thrived on danger. Perhaps that's why he married Rachel,' she added sourly.

'You don't like her, then?' Meagan knew she shouldn't encourage gossip, but she was intensely curious about Cameron's relationship with Rachel. A natural curiosity, she told herself, and anyway she knew she could trust Jessie.

'It's not that I don't like her. But I can't say I approve of the way she's treated Cameron and little Ian…' Jessie stopped, seemingly aware she had said more than she should.

Meagan leaned closer. 'What do you mean?'

'She had an affair—that's why she and Cameron divorced. She met someone wealthier than Cameron. I imagine being Lady Rachel and living up here wasn't what she had expected it to be, and I guess she thought her lover could provide the jet-set life she thought she was getting when she married Cameron.'

'Cameron must have been devastated,' Meagan responded, wondering how a man like Cameron would feel about being betrayed by someone he loved. Perhaps they had more in common than she'd thought.

'I think it was her abandonment of Ian that hurt him most. Cameron would never put his own needs above that of his child, and he couldn't understand how Rachel could risk losing her son. On the other hand, he was happy that she handed over custody of Ian to him.'

How could any woman give up her family? Meagan was thinking. How she would have loved to be in Rachel's shoes, with an adorable son and a husband who loved her. It seemed that now Jessie had started, she was determined to go on.

'Rachel doesn't seem to care for her son. Not the

way most mothers do. As far as I can tell, she uses him simply as a way to Cameron.' Then she looked aghast. 'I'm sorry, Meagan. Please, forgive me. I have no business discussing the family's affairs. Just forget I said anything. Its just—'

'Go on,' said a quiet voice behind them. The two women whirled round. Engrossed, neither of them had heard Cameron come in. Meagan felt herself go red. What on earth must he be thinking? she wondered. Finding the pair of them discussing him and his relationship with his ex-wife.

'Just what is it, Jessie, that you have no business telling Meagan?' Cameron persisted. He narrowed his eyes.

Jessie sprang to her feet.

'Rachel. She shouldn't be living apart from her son,' she said fiercely. 'That child needs a mother.'

'What Rachel chooses to do is up to her. But—' his gaze softened '—you are right. Every child deserves two parents. And it's up to the parents to make that happen—both parents.'

'But if she won't live here?' Jessie persisted.

'Then perhaps I'll have to move back to

London,' Cameron said. 'But whatever Rachel and I decide to do, it's up to us. For the time being, please don't bore Meagan with my problems.'

Meagan could still feel the heat in her face. At the same time she was dismayed at the thought of Cameron returning to London. Why she should, she had no idea. It would be far better that they live miles apart. Maybe then she'd get him out of her system. Horrified at the direction her thoughts were taking, she stood up.

'Thanks for the tea, Jessie, but I should let you get on.'

'You're welcome,' Jessie said. 'You haven't forgotten the ball? Simon—Cameron's younger brother—and a few of his friends are arriving the Friday before.' And Meagan caught her small smile and dreamy look.

So that's the way the land lay. She hoped her new friend wasn't laying herself open to have her heart broken. Of course, Meagan hadn't met this Simon, but if he was anything like his brother, Meagan worried for Jessie.

'I'm looking forward to it,' Meagan said. 'Although I'm still not sure what to wear.'

'Rachel offered you something,' Cameron said, sweeping his eyes over Meagan like a pro. 'You're about the same size, although I think you're about an inch or two shorter.'

'I would lend you something,' Jessie said, eyeing Meagan's figure enviously, 'but I doubt I have anything that'll fit. No, I'm afraid Rachel is your best bet.'

'Rachel left this morning,' Cameron said. 'She won't be back until the day of the ball. However, I'm sure she won't mind if you help yourself to something from her wardrobe.'

Meagan was aghast. 'I couldn't possibly,' she said, shaking her head firmly. It was bad enough that she coveted Rachel's ex-husband, without borrowing her clothes too.

'Tell you what,' Jessie said thoughtfully. 'There's a lovely little boutique in Stornoway— I know you have a few weeks but we could take a trip up there this afternoon.' Jessie brightened at the thought. 'I could do with getting myself some bits and pieces, and it would be nice to have a day out. We could take Ian and Effie.'

'Sounds like a good idea,' Cameron said. 'While you two are organising that, I'm off to check on the fences. Someone phoned to say there was a break near the east perimeter. And Simon's weekend guests are hoping for some shooting, aren't they, Jessie?'

'Mmm, and fishing too. I expect you'll be joining them?'

'Too right,' said Cameron. 'Apart from the fishing I'm looking forward to seeing Simon again. How long is it since he was last here?'

Jessie blushed. 'Five weeks.' She attempted an airy wave that fooled no one. 'But who's counting?'

In the end, Jessie, Meagan, Effie and Ian all clambered into Meagan's Land Rover for the short ferry trip and drive into town. The children were excited at the prospect of a day out, but had promised to be on their best behaviour, which would be rewarded with ice cream sundaes in a café. True to their word, they sat patiently in the dress shop, albeit giggling at Meagan as she tried on numerous totally unsuitable dresses.

Jessie was searching through a row of gowns. Every so often she would pull one out, hold it up against Meagan then with a click of her tongue return it to the rail. Eventually she pulled out a floor-length dress of shimmering deep green silk.

'This is it!' she said excitedly. 'This one matches your eyes perfectly. Go on. Try it on.'

Meagan eyed the gown suspiciously. It looked a little too low cut for her liking, but to keep Jessie happy she tried the dress on. The silk fabric fell about her body and she could feel the fabric cling to her body. Jessie was right—it did match her eyes. And she did feel like a million dollars. Jessie wolf whistled.

'You look stunning,' she said. 'Every eye on the room will be on you.' Casting a look back at the children to make sure they couldn't hear her, she added. 'That will annoy Rachel no end. Sorry, sorry,' she said as she caught Meagan's warning look. 'No more bitchiness—I promise.'

Meagan resisted the urge to pick up their discussion where they had left it earlier that day.

She twirled, enjoying the sensuous feel of the fabric against her skin.

'Now all we need to do,' Jessie said smugly, 'is find matching shoes and a bag.'

Meagan looked over at the two children, who had begun to wriggle with boredom.

'After we have that ice cream we promised, I think,' she said.

Ian skipped over to her and wrapped his small arms around her legs.

'I like you being here,' he said simply. Meagan swallowed the lump in her throat.

'C'mon, then, guys, let's get out of here!'

The days on Uist passed almost too quickly for Meagan. Every morning she saw her patients, then after that she and Cameron would divide the visits between them, before meeting back at the surgery to discuss and review that day's patients.

Mostly the patients Meagan saw were straight-forward to diagnose. The usual colds and flu. There were trickier cases, too, where patients had to be referred to one of the hospitals on the mainland. Every now and again Meagan would consult with Cameron to confirm a diagnosis or to decide a treatment plan. He was never impatient with her and often at the end of the day he would have an informal teaching session. Soon they had settled into the easy understanding of two colleagues who respected each other.

One Thursday there were no visits for either

Cameron or Meagan. Cameron surprised her by suggesting that conditions were perfect for the sail he had promised her.

'There's still a good couple of hours of decent light and you promised to show off your sailing skills,' he teased her. 'When you live here, at the mercy of the elements, you need to make the most of any opportunity.'

Looking out the window, Meagan had to agree. The conditions would be challenging for the average sailor, but for her they were a delight. But could she really spend time alone with Cameron? Although they were getting on as colleagues, spending time together out of work was another matter.

'Another time perhaps?' she said coolly. 'We don't want any gossip.'

'Gossip?' Cameron said quietly. He looked grim for a moment. 'I can't always live my life here worried about gossip. In any case, what would be so strange about two colleagues going sailing? Colin and I go all the time. But if it worries you…'

Meagan returned the challenge in Cameron's eyes.

'You'll get wet. Very wet, if I have my way,' she warned him

'You should know by now an islander is never worried about getting wet.' He grinned. 'Anyway, the last time we were out, it was you who got wet, I seem to recall.'

The memory reminded Meagan that she had been planning to get her revenge. She was curious to see how the macho Dr Stuart coped. When a boat was set to the wind Meagan could make it soar across the water. However, travelling at speed often meant a dip in the ocean. Mostly there would be rescue boats to help in case of a capsize, but out here they would be on their own. It was essential that her sailing partner knew not to panic. She had seen enough to know that Cameron fell into this category.

'OK. You're on,' she said. 'Meet me at the boat in thirty minutes.'

Meagan hurried home and quickly changed into the dry suit she had brought with her. She'd had enough of being wet through, and once the boat was going at speed another drenching was inevitable. It took her slightly longer than usual to squeeze herself into her suit—the effect of all those scones and sandwiches the patients and Jessie kept offering her, she mused ruefully.

She pulled on a waterproof on top of her dry suit and tied her hair back. She was ready.

She was checking over the boat when Cameron arrived. He was in the waterproofs he had worn for the rescue and looked fit and tanned.

'I'll take her out,' Meagan suggested. 'I think I can remember the channel to follow.'

As soon as they were out in clear water, Meagan set the sails. 'OK, this time I'm helmsman and you're crew. Are you ready for this?'

Within seconds the boat was travelling at speed. The wind caught the sails and Meagan hooked her feet under the toe strap and eased herself over the side, counterbalancing the cant of the boat with her weight. She revelled in the speed. Oh, how she had missed this.

'Er, don't you think we should slow down a little?' Cameron said nervously.

Meagan pulled the sails in tighter and the boat picked up more speed. For once there was something she could show Cameron.

'Stay in the middle of the boat if you're worried,' she shouted. 'You'll be perfectly safe there.'

Without saying anything, Cameron joined her, copying her position. 'If you can do it, so can I,' he yelled. Then gave a whoop of excitement.

They tacked upwind for the next forty minutes, working as if they had sailed together for years. Eventually, however, Meagan knew that her underused muscles were getting tired. She allowed the boat to bear away from the wind, letting it slow to a more sedate pace.

'That was fantastic,' Cameron said as the decrease in speed allowed them to talk without shouting. 'I've been around boats all my life but I have never sailed like that.' He looked at her appraisingly. 'When did you learn to sail?'

'My father took me out on his boat from the age of four. I always loved it. I was in the sailing team at university— If you remember, I was with them when we met. There was a chance of being selected for the pre-Olympic training squad, but I turned it down. I chose to study for my finals instead.'

'Do you regret it?' Cameron asked.

Meagan thought for a moment. 'I suppose life is full of choices. We make the best decisions we can at the time. Sometimes they work out, sometimes they don't.'

She thought about the decisions she had made. Marrying Charlie, putting off having children, becoming a doctor. Did she regret marrying Charlie? Maybe and maybe not. They'd had some good times, and as the pain was receding she could remember more of the happier times and fewer of the bad ones. And her decision to come here? She allowed her gaze to linger on the open sea, the small uninhabited islands and the man in front of her, with his laughing brown eyes, sexy body and love of life. If she hadn't come, she might never have seen him again, and the thought scared her. The realisation made her look away in confusion. The way she felt about this man, the way she had felt about him from the first moment she had seen him had never changed. He still made her heart pound and her knees go weak, in a way no other man had before or since. She loved being with him. When she wasn't with him, she missed him. The truth was, she loved him. He was her soul mate and she had known it from the moment they had met. But how did he feel about her? Did he feel anything for her except friendship?

'What about you?' she asked. 'Do you have regrets?'

'I find its pointless thinking that way. We take the hand we are dealt and make the most of it.'

What did that mean? Meagan wondered. Was he thinking of Rachel? Did he regret marrying her, or the divorce?

As if he'd read her thoughts, he went on, 'One thing I'll never regret is my son. But I am sorry that he doesn't see his mother as often as he should. A child needs his mother.'

'And his father,' Meagan added. She paused, feeling the familiar stab of pain. She shook it off. As Cameron had said, you took the hand you were dealt.

The wind had driven the last of the clouds from the sky. The breeze had dropped suddenly and the boat was barely moving. Without the wind and the clouds the sun was hot. Meagan removed her waterproof then, as the sun continued to toast her shoulders, unzipped her dry suit and peeled the top down over her hips. She was glad she'd thought to put her bikini on underneath.

Cameron watched her through lidded eyes before he too removed his waterproofs. He carried on stripping down to his jeans and T-shirt, then with a last look at Meagan removed his T-shirt. Meagan held her breath. Surely he was going to stop there. She averted her eyes from his muscular bronzed chest, but was unable to stop herself remembering the feel of his skin on hers, the strength of his arms as he had held her all these years ago. She wondered what it would be like to find herself in his arms again. She forced her thoughts away from the image. It was too dangerous—and pointless—to let her mind go in that direction.

'Do you fancy a swim?' Cameron said. 'See that island to your left? It's not too far. The wind is unlikely to pick up for a couple of hours yet. We could anchor here and swim across.'

Thinking that a dip was exactly what she needed to cool her overheated imagination, Meagan grinned as he dropped the anchor. Removing her dry suit completely, she stood on the side of the boat poised to dive. 'Race you,' she said as she plunged into the water.

She gasped as the cold water enveloped her. Without waiting to see if Cameron was following, she struck out for shore. She was almost there when she felt a hand on her ankle. She trod water.

'Do you think I'm going to be beaten by a woman?' Cameron said. He set off again with sure strokes, leaving her in his wake. He beat her easily, and was waiting for her just offshore.

'Hey, you cheated,' she said. 'What kind of gentleman does that?'

'I never said I was a gentleman,' he said, grinning.

Meagan splashed him and soon they were tussling in the water. Meagan felt his hands around her waist as he lifted her into the air. He held her there for a moment and they looked into each other's eyes. Cameron's darkened with desire. He lowered Meagan until he held her in front of his body. Although Cameron was standing, it was too deep for Meagan's feet to touch the bottom. Still holding her firmly by the waist, he lowered his head and covered her mouth with his. Meagan felt a flame of desire shoot through her body and before she could help herself she wrapped her legs around his hips.

She could feel his response through his jeans and it heightened her own desire. They were kissing frantically as Cameron walked Meagan still wrapped around him towards the beach. She could feel his hands on her back, on her bottom, searching—feeling—sending shock waves of pleasure through her nerve endings. He dropped his mouth and pushing aside her bikini top with his lips found her nipple. As he licked and nibbled her breast Meagan arched her back, allowing him better access.

As he lowered her onto the damp sand, his thumbs reached under her bikini bottom, touching and teasing until Meagan could almost bear it no longer.

'Please, Cameron,' she gasped.

'What about protection?' he said.

'It's all right,' she replied. 'You don't have to worry.'

He pulled away from her, and she watched him remove his saturated jeans, which clung to him and revealed the full extent of his desire. Then he was beside her and her bikini was off.

As his hands explored every inch of her body, Meagan moaned with pleasure. It felt as if every nerve in her body was on fire. Desperate to feel him inside her, she raked his back with her nails, pulling him on top of her, opening her legs to allow him easy entry. He pulled back, enjoying her surrender, before he plunged into her. As Meagan climaxed with a shudder he flipped her on top of him and within moments had her riding the top of the wave once more. This time they came together. They collapsed in each other's arms, gasping for breath. But Cameron hadn't finished with her yet. Once again Meagan felt her body respond to his touch. This time he was slower, bringing her almost to the point of no return before stopping then waiting a couple of seconds and then starting again. Just as she thought she'd have to beg he took her once more and with a couple of deep strokes took her with him once more to orgasm.

They lay in each other's arms, sated. The breeze licked Meagan's skin and she was aware of the tiny grains of sand that seemed to be hiding in every crease of her body. She didn't want to move, scared that she'd break the spell. Cameron raised himself on his elbow and looked at her.

'Cold?' he said softly. 'Come on, we'd better think about getting back,'

'Can't we just stay here?' Meagan replied. 'Forget about the rest of the world? Anyway, I don't think I could move—my muscles feel like jelly.'

He pulled her into his arms. 'Just for a few more minutes then we'd better be getting back.'

Meagan trailed a lazy finger across his chest.

'Tell me about you and Rachel,' she said softly. She could feel the tension in Cameron's body as soon as she mentioned his ex wife's name.

'There's not much to tell,' he said slowly. 'I met Rachel when I was studying in London. We dated, but eventually we—I broke it off. I think I realised that we didn't really have that much in common.' He looked into the distance, his eyes bleak.

'I met you shortly after Rachel and I broke up. I was spending the summer with my family on Uist.'

Meagan felt a surge of relief. So he hadn't been with Rachel when he had met her. She would have hated it if he had been with her while involved with someone else. It would have cheapened that night for her for ever.

'But you must have changed your mind about breaking up with Rachel,' Meagan persisted. 'You married her. Had a child together.' A sneaking suspicion was forming in Meagan's mind.

'I meant what I said when we met. I planned to contact you just as soon as I could.'

'But you didn't,' Meagan said flatly. 'I never heard from you, not a word. I even wondered if something had happened to you.' She drew a painful breath. At least that was what she had thought at first. She had been so sure he would contact her that she had imagined the worst. She had wondered if he were ill, or even—she shuddered at the memory—dead. And she'd had no way to get in touch with him. She hadn't known much about him apart from the fact that he worked in London. That was all. And then, just when she'd been going out of her mind with worry and about to phone every hospital in London to ask if they had a Cameron working there, she had caught a glimpse of him one weekend when she had been visiting friends.

Just the briefest sight, but enough to know he was perfectly well. It was then she had realised that her dream of being with him had been just that.

Cameron pulled her closer. 'I'm sorry. It didn't occur to me that you'd think something had happened to me. I just assumed you'd think me a bastard and move on with your life.'

'You still haven't told me *why*,' Meagan said. However painful it was, she needed to know. 'Was it because you're titled? Were you expected to marry someone more appropriate than a doctor?'

'There was an element of that,' Cameron said slowly. 'I expected some opposition from my father, but I never have and never will do anything except follow my own path. That wouldn't have stopped me. Besides, my parents always knew that the title in itself means little to me. It's the responsibilities of the title that go with it. Looking after the estate for everyone, not least the community, is what is important. The social status of having a title, means nothing to me.'

'Go on,' Meagan said.

'The day after you and I met, Rachel flew up

to Uist. It was a shock. She hadn't told me she was coming. I thought it was a last-ditch attempt to try and get back together and I was about to tell her it was useless, that I had met someone else, when she dropped her bombshell. She was pregnant—with my child.'

Meagan squeezed her eyes against the familiar ache.

'And so you did the honourable thing?' Meagan said softly.

'I had no choice, She said if I wouldn't marry her, she would terminate the pregnancy.' Cameron's voice held the echo of the anguish he had felt.

'She wanted to marry you despite not really wanting your child?' Meagan said. How could any woman think like that? If Rachel had loved Cameron enough to want to marry him, surely she would have wanted his baby?

'I don't think Rachel ever truly loved me,' Cameron went on, answering Meagan's unspoken question. 'It was the idea of being Lady Grimsay she loved.' He laughed but there was little humour in the sound. 'I think she assumed when we got married we would live in London and spend all our time socialising.'

'But you married her nevertheless? Knowing she didn't love you? Knowing that she was the kind of woman who would end a pregnancy because she didn't get her own way?'

'I told you I had no option. I couldn't take the risk that she'd carry out her threat. I wanted my child.'

'Why didn't you tell me at least?'

'There was no point. I could have come to you and told you. I couldn't have done it over the phone, but I knew if I saw you I might not be able to go through with the marriage.'

'So you married a woman you didn't love. Someone who was more suited to the role of being Lady Grimsay?' Meagan couldn't help keep the bitterness from her voice.

'I was fond of her. I thought it was enough to make the marriage work. I thought that once we were a family, it would be different.'

'Then what happened?' Meagan said into the silence.

'Rachel wanted us to live in London. So we moved there. I completed my specialist training and started looking for a consultant post. But then she started getting modelling jobs.

Eventually she was travelling all over the world, and I was looking after Ian with the help of a string of nannies. It was hopeless. My son was hardly seeing either of his parents. I missed being here but more importantly I was missing seeing my son grow up. Then Rachel met someone else. I could hardly blame her. I was never at home and when I was I was too tired to go out to parties with her. And I thought that we should be spending any spare time at home— together—as a family.'

Gently Cameron disengaged himself from Meagan and started pulling on his jeans. Mutely Meagan started getting dressed too. She shivered and it wasn't just from the gathering coolness in the air. Cameron stood apart from her as if he was already beginning to regret making love to her.

'The final straw came before her affair. I told her I wanted us all to move back here. My mother had died and my father was getting frailer. He needed my help. Rachel was furious. She wasn't prepared to give up her city lifestyle to live here. Then I found about the affair.' His mouth twisted. 'He was very rich, much richer than an impoverished Scottish lord whose main income came from his salary as a GP. We agreed to divorce and that I would move back here with Ian. It made sense. He'll be Lord Grimsay one day, with all the responsibilities that entails. We agreed that Rachel would come and see him whenever she could. But in the meantime he'd have stability in a community that knows and loves him.'

He moved towards Meagan. 'Rachel's lover never did marry her, and she discovered that there were elements of being Lady Grimsay that she missed. She wanted us to give it another go. So, you see, It's all a bit of a mess. But there is one thing I'll never regret—and that's my son. He's the most important thing in my life.'

How lucky Rachel was and she seemed to have no idea. Meagan would have given anything to have had a child and had she been given the chance, she would never have allowed anything or anybody to take that child away from her. The pain she felt at losing her chance of a baby was still intense. Would it ever fade? she wondered.

Cameron must have seen something in her expression. 'What about you?' he asked. 'Did you and your husband not want children—or were you not ready yet?' Meagan looked up at the sky and watched the clouds for a moment.

'I fell pregnant,' she said 'but at eight weeks I had to have emergency surgery for an ectopic pregnancy in one of my Fallopian tubes.' Cameron stepped closer, drawing her into his arms.

'I was devastated—we both were. And what was worse was they discovered my other tube was also damaged. So I am unlikely ever to have children.' She felt her voice break as she remembered how she had felt when they had told her the news.

'Charlie always wanted a big family. Although he said it didn't matter, I knew it did. And then I…' She broke off and took a breath before continuing. 'I threw myself into my work. I guess from then on we just drifted apart. We spent hardly any time together. We were like strangers.'

She stopped for a moment letting the memories wash over her. She remembered coming into their empty flat, leaving before Charlie was up, how their sex life had dwindled away to nothing. They had hardly spoken. Oh, he had tried at first, but she had been too wrapped up in her own pain to notice his.

'And then,' she went on in a rush, wanting to tell him everything, 'one day I got a phone call. Charlie had been driving to a conference and his car had swerved to miss a car on the wrong side of the road. He was killed instantly. I never got the chance to say goodbye, that I was sorry.' She felt her eyes fill with tears and her throat tightened. 'He wasn't alone in the car. He was with a colleague—a nurse—who was going to the same conference. She escaped with a few minor injuries. She came to see me after the funeral, told me they had been in love and that he hadn't known how to tell me. It was the deceit of his affair that almost destroyed me. Why couldn't he have told me the truth? I would have let him go. I knew I didn't love him and I would have wanted him to be happy. I felt so guilty. It wasn't fair. Just because I couldn't have children, I shouldn't have made both our lives a misery. I should have encouraged him to leave.'

Cameron pulled Meagan back down on the sand and she buried her head in his shoulder.

'After the funeral I ran away. I wanted to be where no one knew me. Oh, I loved my time with Médecins Sans Frontières but I'm not proud of the reason I took the job.'

'And now?' Cameron prompted gently. 'How do you feel now?'

Meagan closed her eyes as she thought for a moment. How *did* she honestly feel now? she wondered. She had spent the last few years feeling torn by Charlie's affair, and the happiness he had missed out on. Now with sudden clarity she realised she had been burying her grief—for her lost child, for the babies she would never have, for the failure of a marriage that had begun with so much love and promise—behind a wall of anger and resentment. Putting all the blame on Charlie, when she was just as much to blame for the breakdown of their marriage. It had been easier for her to keep the anger simmering rather than acknowledging the pain and grief she feared would overwhelm her.

'Charlie thought it would break my heart if I found out he was with another woman. But he was *wrong*. I would have been glad for him. I realise that now.' She turned to Cameron. 'Isn't that so sad? How we think that by not being honest with people we're protecting them when all we're doing is hurting them and ourselves more.' She sat up and hugged her knees, suddenly feeling as if a huge weight had been lifted off her shoulders. Charlie had been denied a happy ending, and for that she'd always feel partially responsible, but that didn't mean she should deny herself one too. 'I feel as if I have the chance to start my life over,' she said. 'Coming here, meeting you again. It's as if fate—'

'Meagan, don't.' Cameron interrupted softly, disengaging himself from her embrace. She looked up at him. Something seemed to shut down in his eyes.

Oh, God, why had she said that when it was obvious he didn't feel the same way about her? For a moment they sat in silence, lost in their own thoughts.

'If we stay much longer, they'll send the coast-guard out looking for us.' He held out his hand and pulled her to her feet. 'I don't know about you, but I have spent too much time in their company already this week.'

Was that all he was going to say? Meagan wondered. But, then, what else had she expected? A proposal? Just because they'd had the most amazing sex, it didn't mean they were getting married. They should take things slowly. Get to know each other. See if they had more in common than just lust. But even as she thought the words, Meagan knew she was kidding herself. She had never stopped loving him. She found her bikini and pulled it on. She loved Cameron. Against her better judgement. But it was too late. For better or worse, she knew she would love him until the breath left her body. But how did he feel about her? He had said that Rachel wanted him back. Was she going to have her heart broken again? This time Meagan knew there would be no way back.

Cameron turned to her. 'There's one more thing I have to tell you,' he said. 'When Rachel agreed to get a divorce and let Ian come back here with me, she made me promise her I'd never get married again.'

'But that's ridiculous,' Meagan burst out. 'She had no right to make you promise anything of the sort.'

'The trouble is she swore that if I ever did, she would fight me for custody of Ian. She knows that I would never allow anyone to take him away from me.'

'But she'd never win custody,' Meagan protested. 'He spends all his time with you.'

'That's just it. He doesn't spend all his time with me. He spends a large part of his time with Mrs McLeod and Jessie. You know what kind of hours I work. And she would have no compunction about using my domestic arrangements to argue that custody should be given to her. So you may be right,' he said, 'but I'm afraid that is a risk I am just not prepared to take.'

And as they made preparations to leave the beach, Meagan knew that she could never make him choose between her and his child.

CHAPTER SEVEN

DESPITE the sun still being high in the sky, Meagan felt a distinct chill in her heart. They swam back to the boat, raised anchor and set sail for home. Although the wind had picked up enough to use the sails, the late afternoon sunshine was still warm and Cameron stayed in his jeans and Meagan in her bikini. As she held the tiller, Meagan sneaked glances at Cameron. Every time she looked at him she felt her heart thrill. How she would love him to stay with her tonight. Maybe, despite the promise he had made to Rachel, they could just enjoy whatever time they had together. For a moment she let herself imagine the two of them snuggling in front of the fire against the evening chill, and then… She felt a shiver of desire. She wanted him again. He must have felt her eyes on him because he looked up and catching her eye, smiled bleakly. She felt her heart sink. Would she be prepared to sneak around, hiding their relationship from everyone? Immediately she knew the answer. If Cameron wasn't free to love her, openly and proudly, she couldn't be with him.

As they approached the bay, Meagan could see that there was someone standing outside her house, shielded eyes looking out to sea. Catching a shimmer of red she recognised the figure as Jessie. She could see from the way Jessie was pacing that something was wrong. She felt a flicker of anxiety. Was something wrong with Effie?

Cameron noticed Jessie at the same time. He stood, pulling on his T-shirt. 'Something's up,' he said. Quickly he took down the sails. He jumped out leaving Meagan to finish sorting out the boat. As she worked she watched Jessie run towards Cameron. She was gesticulating and clearly agitated. Moments later Cameron jumped into his car and sped off.

Hastily, Meagan finished securing the boat and ran towards Jessie.

'What is it, Jessie? What's wrong?'

'It's Ian. He was complaining of stomach pain this morning. I wasn't too bothered at first. I thought he had probably caught the same bug Effie had. But now he's in real pain. I think it's more serious. When I couldn't get hold of Cameron, I tried the practice in the south, but I couldn't get them either. Then I came down here just as you were coming back in.' The words came out in a rush.

'I'll just grab my bag, Jessie. Then I'll go back with you to Grimsay House.' As she spoke, she ran towards her house, Jessie following. Once there, Meagan darted into her bedroom and pulled a pair of jeans and a top over her bikini. Scooping up her medical bag, she took a distressed Jessie by the arm.

'C'mon, Jessie,' she said, ushering her into her car. 'Try not to worry. Kids can seem very ill and then the next minute they're as right as rain.'

But she could see that Jessie wasn't convinced. In a few minutes they were inside Grimsay House. Meagan followed Jessie as she ran up to Ian's room. There they found Cameron examining his son, a worried look on his face. He turned towards Meagan, frowning.

'I think it's appendicitis. In fact, I know it's appendicitis.'

Ian, his little face pinched, moaned softly.

'I want Mummy, Daddy. Where is my mummy?'

'Shh, my darling. She's in London. She'd be here if she could. In the meantime, you have to be a brave boy and let Daddy look after you.'

As he looked away from his son, Meagan could see anguish written all over his face. She touched his shoulder. He flinched away from her touch as if he'd been burnt. She dropped her hand to her side.

'Let me look at him, Cameron,' she said quietly.

Cameron stood aside while Meagan examined the little boy. When Ian cried out when she pressed the right side of his abdomen, she knew that Cameron's initial diagnosis was correct.

She took Cameron by the arm and, leaving Jessie to comfort the boy, took Cameron to one side.

'I agree,' she said. 'It's appendicitis. What do you want to do?'

'He needs surgery,' Cameron said. He pulled a hand through his thick dark hair and Meagan's heart went out to him. She longed to put her arms around him and comfort him, but here in front of his child wasn't the place.

'Have we time to send him to Stornoway?' she asked.

'I don't think so,' Cameron replied. 'I think we should go ahead and operate at the hospital.'

'In that case, I'll do the surgery,' Meagan said firmly. 'Could you get hold of someone to anaesthetise?'

Cameron looked at Meagan. 'I don't know. Maybe we should get him airlifted to Glasgow? They have surgeons there who do this every day of the week.'

He didn't trust her to operate on his son, even after all they had been through. But could she blame him? They were talking about his child. But neither could he operate on Ian. A doctor needed a certain distance from his patient.

'If you think there is time, yes,' she said. 'That's what we will do.'

Cameron rubbed his jaw. It was the first time she had seen him look indecisive.

'Cameron,' she said, 'whatever we decide to do, we need to make a decision *now*.'

'You've examined him. What do you think?'

'I think the risk of waiting until we get him to Glasgow is far greater than operating here. The surgery is fairly routine. I can handle it, Cameron. I would tell you if I had any doubts. I told you before, emergency surgery is where I have a lot of practice. You have to believe me when I say I have more surgical experience than general practice.'

'But what if there are complications? No disrespect to you but anything could happen. If the appendix ruptures before we remove it, he could die.'

'And the longer we wait, the greater chance there is of that happening.'

Cameron stared at his son for one long moment. He seemed to make up his mind.

'Let's call in the air ambulance. They'll be able to give us a rough time of arrival. In the meantime, let's get the theatre in Benbecula organised. That way, if it looks as if his condition is deteriorating rapidly, we can go ahead with surgery.'

'That sounds like a plan. Let's get going.' Meagan turned to Ian, crouching by his side.

'Ian, you need an operation on your tummy,'

Meagan said. 'It won't hurt because you will be fast asleep. But we need to get you to a hospital so we can do the operation. Do you understand?'

'Are you going to do it, Daddy?' the little boy asked his father.

'No, *mo ghaol*,' his father said. 'It's not a good idea for fathers to operate on their little boys. But, I'll be right next to you all the time. And I'll be there when you wake up.

'Will Mummy be there too?'

Cameron shook his head. Meagan could see from the way he clenched his jaw that he was trying hard not to let his child see his pain. Tears filled Ian's eyes.

'I wish Mummy never had to go away, Daddy. If you were still married, she'd always be here when I need her, wouldn't she?'

'I'm going to phone her and I know she'll want to be with you as soon as she can. She loves you very much—you know that, don't you?'

Cameron squatted next to Ian and pulled him into his arms. He whispered something in his ear. Whatever it was, it seemed to have the right effect. Ian smiled and relaxed into his father's embrace.

'Could you phone the hospital, Meagan, and the air ambulance?' Cameron said, lifting his son in his arms. 'I'll take him to the hospital in my car. Luckily the hospital is near the airport. We need someone standing by ready to anaethetise. I'll get them on my mobile.'

'OK. I'll be right behind you,' Meagan said. She touched his shoulder. 'It's going to be all right,' she said gently.

Cameron looked right through her.

'Jessie, could you keep trying to get hold of Rachel? Tell her I'll let her know what's happening as soon as I can.'

Meagan let her hand drop. He was distraught and who could blame him? In the meantime, she had a job to do.

By the time Meagan arrived at the hospital, Ian's condition had deteriorated.

'The air ambulance is on its way,' she told Cameron, 'but it will be a couple of hours before they get here. Then it will be another while before they get him to hospital.' She looked at Cameron. 'I don't think we should wait.'

'I don't know,' said Cameron.

'Look, 'Meagan said, 'the longer we wait the more likely it is that he'll have complications. It's a pretty straightforward op. If we do it now.'

Cameron sighed. He looked shaken. 'OK. Let's do it.' He turned to Meagan and grasped her by the shoulders. She could feel his fingers biting into her through the thin fabric of her blouse.

'I've got to trust you. You can't let me down. If anything happens to Ian, I…' He tailed off, unable to complete the sentence.

'I won't let anything happen. I promise. I wouldn't do this if I didn't know I could. Now, you stay with Ian while I get changed and scrub up.'

'I'm coming in too,' he said.

'Do you think that's wise? You'd be better waiting. I'll let you know when I'm finished.'

Cameron looked at her, his mouth set in a grim line. 'I am going to be in theatre with my son. Please, don't argue with me about this.'

'OK, then. But you have to promise to stay out of the way.'

In the end the operation was straightforward. While she was operating she could feel

Cameron's eyes on her every move. She knew he was prepared to take over should she show the slightest hesitation or uncertainty. She pushed away the thought that she was operating on the son of the man she loved to the back of her mind. Once she started operating, everything else around her disappeared as she concentrated.

Finally the inflamed appendix was out. Looking at it, Meagan knew they had made the right decision not to delay. Even an hour more and the appendix could have ruptured. As it was, Ian should make a good recovery.

Cameron held Ian's hand throughout the procedure. Over his mask she could see the relief in his eyes as she began to close.

When she had finished, Ian was wheeled into the recovery area. He was beginning to come round, although Meagan knew it would be a little while before he was fully conscious. Once he had come round he would need a couple of days in hospital.

One of the nurses came through. 'Dr Stuart, we have your wife on the phone. I've brought her up to speed, but she still wants to speak to you.'

Reluctantly Cameron stood up, releasing his son's hand. 'Tell her I'll be there in a minute.'

He turned to Meagan. The lines of worry were still there, but she could see that he knew the worst was over.

'Thank you,' he said, his voice gruff with emotion. 'I should never have doubted you. You did a fine job.'

'All in a day's work.' Meagan smiled at him, although now that the operation was over she felt her knees shake.

Cameron leaned over Ian and kissed him. 'I'll be back in a minute,' he promised the sleeping child. He was back in minutes. Ian was beginning to open his eyes.

'Daddy?' he said as he saw his father. 'Am I fixed?'

'You are going to be fine,' Cameron said. 'A few days in bed and then you'll be up and about.'

'Mummy?' Ian asked, his eyes searching the room.

'She's on her way. She'll be here before you know it. And she won't leave you again. I promise.'

'Will you and Dr Galbraith stay with me until Mummy comes?'

Over the top of Ian's head Cameron looked at Meagan. She didn't need to see the message there.

'I'll stay as long as you and your daddy need me to, Ian,' Meagan promised. 'Now, try and get some sleep.

During the next few days Meagan saw little of Cameron. When he wasn't at work he was spending his spare time with Ian. Meagan knew that Rachel had returned, but didn't see her either. Jessie had rung her one evening, suggesting they go for a bar supper, and had told her that Rachel was back and also spending time with her son.

'Ian asks for you all the time,' Jessie told Meagan. 'He seems to have taken quite a shine to you.'

Meagan hadn't seen Ian since he'd been discharged from hospital. It was his mother he needed by his side. Not her.

The day after Ian had left hospital Cameron had come to see her. She had just finished her evening meal, although she hadn't had much of an appetite, and had been lighting the fire in the sitting room when a knock had come on the door.

When she'd opened it to find Cameron standing there, her heart had thumped. He'd looked divine in a crisp white shirt open at the neck and pale chinos.

'Hi, there,' she said softly, not even attempting to hide the pleasure she felt at seeing him.

'Can I come in?' he asked.

As she moved aside to let him come in she caught a whiff of his aftershave that sent her pulse racing with the memories of the last time she had been close to him.

'I can't stay long,' he said. 'They're expecting me back at the house.' Meagan felt a stab of disappointment. She couldn't help it, but she wanted more than a few minutes alone with him. Still, even a short time together was better than nothing.

But as he refused her offer of a seat and coffee, she could see that something was wrong. He looked uncomfortable, almost as if being with her was the last place he wanted to be.

'Is everything all right?' she asked.

'I need to speak to you.'

'Well, then,' she said, trying to ignore the tendrils of dread that were beginning to wrap themselves around her heart. 'Don't you think you'd better sit down?'

He sat in her chair near the fire, his large frame almost dwarfing the sitting room. He clasped his hands together and rested them on his knees.

'Rachel and I have decided to marry again,' he blurted suddenly.

Meagan felt her blood run cold.

'Oh?' was all she could manage.

'She's been offered a modelling contract in New York. It's very lucrative and is likely to lead to a higher profile in the modelling world. It's her big break.' Cameron's mouth twisted.

'She is going to take it, but wants Ian to go too. And me. That is… Oh, hell.' He pulled a hand through his hair.

It needs a trim, Meagan thought incongruously.

'She wants us to be a family again.'

'And what do you want?' Meagan asked through frozen lips.

'I want to be with my son. I want my son to have two loving parents who are with him all the time. Apart from that, it doesn't matter what else I want.' He stood up and started pacing around the room. It only took a couple of strides before he was forced to turn around and go the other way.

'And us, Cameron? What about us?'

'There can be no us,' he said flatly.

'I see,' Meagan said, although she didn't— not really.

'For God's sake, Meagan. I need you to under-stand. I don't love Rachel, not the way I—' He broke off. 'Not the way she wants. But seeing my son ill, needing his mother and her not being there, was more than I could bear. I don't think adults have the right to put their own needs above those of their child.'

'And what about Rachel? Isn't that what she's doing?'

'Rachel will always do what she wants. I know that. But at the moment she holds the cards. If she wants to go, I can't stop her. And how could I deprive my child of his mother? If he hardly sees her now, he would see even less of her when she is over there. Anyway, it's not an option. She insists that she is taking Ian and that there is not a court in the world that would stop her.'

'So you have made up your mind?'

'Yes,' he said heavily. 'We are going to announce it at the ball. I thought it only fair to warn you in advance.'

'That was thoughtful of you.' Meagan didn't even try to keep the sarcasm from her voice. Now she was beginning to feel angry. What a fool she had been to believe that he had feelings for her. Maybe he had until she had told him she couldn't have children. He probably would have been content to have an affair with her, just as long as it didn't get in the way of what he wanted. Well, she had stood in the path of a man once. She wasn't about to do it again.

'Is that all?' she said, standing and crossing to the door. All she wanted was for him to leave. She needed time on her own to absorb the news and she was damned if she was going to let him see how much he had hurt her.

'Meagan, I…' He stood in front of her and, reaching out, traced her cheekbone with a finger. 'I never meant to hurt you. God knows, you have been hurt enough.'

Meagan smiled bleakly. 'Don't worry, Cameron. I'm a lot tougher than you think. And anyway we both knew it wasn't serious. People have sex these days all the time without it having to mean anything. So you can relax—I have no intention of trying to stop you. Now, don't you think you had better be going?'

The day of the ball looked as if it was going to be fine. The last thing Meagan felt like doing was going. But she had to. Colin and Peggy were returning from Australia today and would be going to the ball. They'd expect to see her there. Everyone would expect to see her there. And, anyway, she thought, squaring her shoulders, she wasn't going to give Rachel the pleasure of knowing how humiliated she felt.

The last couple of weeks had been awful. Seeing Cameron every day, knowing that soon he'd be married to Rachel once more, knowing that very shortly he'd be out of her life for good, was almost unbearable. Pretending that everything was OK, keeping her manner light in front of the staff, had been more difficult than she had expected. She couldn't help it, but every time she saw him, even caught a glimpse of him, her heart somersaulted.

As she dipped her spoon into the lightly boiled egg she had made for breakfast, she was suddenly overcome by a wave of nausea. She only just made it to the bathroom on time. She sat on the bathroom floor, waiting for the nausea to settle. I wonder what caused that? she thought. Maybe she would have a genuine reason not for not going to the ball. But after a few minutes she felt fine. She was brushing her teeth when she heard Jessie's cheery voice call out.

'Hello, hello. Is there a doctor in the house? A corny line, I know, but I always wanted to say that.' She took one look at Meagan and then was concerned.

'Hey, I hope you don't mind me saying, but you look dreadful.'

'Thanks,' Meagan said. 'Those are the words a woman always wants to hear. Don't worry, I'm fine now, although I think I may be coming down with something.'

'Oh, don't say you're going to miss the ball. I'm so looking forward to introducing you to everyone.'

Meagan had to laugh at Jessie's downcast expression.

'I gather the handsome Simon has arrived, then?'

Jessie blushed, then grinned. 'Is it that obvious?' she asked. 'Oh, Meagan, there's no point. He's rich—well, relatively speaking—and titled, and I'm just a cook with a small child to support. It's pointless even thinking about it.'

'You're not just a cook,' Meagan exclaimed. 'You are a beautiful woman who does what she needs to in order to support her child. And, by the way, you are an excellent cook. How many people can say that?'

'True, having tasted your cooking when I came to lunch the other day. I'm afraid I can attest to the fact that you are many things, Meagan Galbraith, but a cook is not one of them.'

The two women laughed and Meagan felt slightly better. One good thing at least had come out of her return to the island. She had made a good friend in Jessie. Then, as the realisation dawned that she wouldn't be here for much longer, her smile faded.

'What is it, Meagan?' Jessie asked.

Meagan shook her head. 'I didn't want to tell you until after the ball but I won't be staying here after all. I've decided a permanent position is not for me. I'll stay, of course, until Colin finds someone else.'

'Oh, Meagan. I'm so sorry. I thought you were happy here. Is it the job? Do you find it boring after the excitement of the big city or working abroad?'

'You're forgetting everything that's happened since I've been here,' Meagan reminded her. 'Air and sea rescues, emergency surgeries. How could I possibly be bored?'

'I am going to miss you so much.' Jessie went over to Meagan and hugged her hard. 'What does Cameron say? I bet he's sorry you are leaving.'

Meagan stiffened. 'I haven't told him yet. And anyway…' Meagan bit her lip. She had been about to tell Jessie about Cameron and Rachel and that he was leaving. But it wasn't her place to tell. A thought struck her. With Cameron gone, Colin would be in a difficult position. It wouldn't be fair to abandon him too. On the other hand, could she stay with all the memories that were here? And when Cameron and Rachel came back on holiday, as they were bound to do? It would be unbearable.

Jessie was looking at Meagan speculatively. 'I know, Meagan.'

Meagan looked at her sharply. 'Know what?'

'I know that Rachel and Cameron are getting married again. And that they'll be going away. He told me.'

Meagan felt a wave of relief. For one moment she had thought that Cameron had told Jessie about them. But as soon as she thought it, she knew that Cameron wasn't that kind of man. He would never share something that wasn't his to share.

'Were you surprised?' Meagan asked.

'Surprised? That's putting it mildly. More like gobsmacked, disbelieving, incredulous. What on earth is he thinking?'

Meagan didn't have to ask—it was clear from not just Jessie's words but her expression what she thought of Cameron's announcement. But still she couldn't resist posing the question. 'You don't approve, then?'

'Approve? How could I? I don't believe for one minute that either of them is in love with the other. If they ever were. I suspect, although Cameron didn't say, that it has something to do with Ian.' Jessie stood up, looked around the room and then sat down again, clearly agitated.

'You don't have feelings for him yourself?' Meagan asked, suddenly curious. How awful that would be.

'Feelings for Cameron,' Jessie replied slowly. 'Of course I have feelings for Cameron. I couldn't love my own brother more than I love that pig-headed man. That's why I'm so annoyed. I've been wishing for years that he would meet the right woman, someone who shared his passions and interests. Someone who would love him to death.' She stopped suddenly. 'Someone very like you, in fact.' She looked closely at Meagan, her green eyes shrewd.

Meagan blushed under Jessie's scrutiny, cursing her inability to hide her feelings.

'Well, well,' Jessie said, giving a low whistle under her breath. 'So that's the way the wind blows, is it?'

It crossed Meagan's mind to lie. But she had never been a good liar.

'Please, Jessie. Keep it to yourself. It's nothing really. And as you said, he's getting married. So there is absolutely no point at all in me having feelings for Cameron.'

'He's even more daft than I gave him credit for if he's ignoring what's under his nose,' Jessie said crossly. 'I just know you two would be perfect together—at the very least you both seem to love nothing more than putting your lives at risk. But now he's insisting on marrying Rachel again. She doesn't even like getting wet. And why? Because he feels guilty about depriving his child of both parents.'

'You have to give him credit for that at least.' Meagan couldn't help sticking up for Cameron. 'I have known so many women whose husbands have just walked out on them and their children. After all, isn't the child the most important person in the relationship?'

'I agree, Meagan, to a point. But Ian has always managed fine with mainly his father around.'

'But has he?' Meagan persisted. 'You heard him when he was ill. He desperately wanted his mother. At the end of the day isn't that what all children want? To be with their mother?'

Jessie shook her head regretfully. 'I suppose,

thinking about it that way, you're right.' Her voice trembled slightly. 'I only wish my child had the luxury of two parents. I've tried to do my best for her, but it would be so much easier if Hamish was still alive.'

'Oh, Jessie.' Meagan took her hand. 'You couldn't help what happened. I guess the difference is that Cameron can do something about it for his child.'

Jessie blew her nose loudly. 'I still think it's not right, though. Two parents are best, but surely only when they love each other. Children are very sensitive like that, you know.'

'Do you ever think you'll marry again?'

This time it was Jessie's turn to blush. 'Aye, well,' she said. 'You never know. But one thing's for sure—I would never marry anyone who wasn't prepared to accept Effie as his own. Not to replace Hamish, you understand—no one could ever do that.' She looked wistful. 'Anyway, so far there haven't been any offers.'

'Is there anyone you wish would offer?' Meagan teased gently, knowing that Simon was back, happy to steer the conversation away from Cameron and herself.

'Maybe. Neither of us have been particularly lucky in love so far, have we? Oh, Meagan, you have to stay. I'll miss you terribly if you go.'

'And I would miss you too.' Impulsively Meagan stood and hugged Jessie. The two women broke apart and Meagan blinked away a tear.

What is wrong with me these days? she thought. I never used to be this emotional.

'Anyway, I'd better go,' Jessie said. 'I've masses to do before tonight. To be fair, they insisted on getting caterers in so I could enjoy the ball, but I want to keep my eye on everything. Mrs McLeod's going to take over from me. God help them if she finds anything that's not quite perfect.'

'How many guests do you have for the weekend?' Meagan asked.

'Around half a dozen. No doubt they'll be wanting something when they come back from the fishing—Cameron has taken them out. And then, of course, it's breakfast and lunch tomorrow before they finally leave.'

'Hard work for you,' Meagan said sympathetically.

'Och, I don't mind. It keeps me out of

mischief. I'll be down later to pick you up and I'll introduce you to everyone. That is, if you don't feel worse!' And then, with a quick kiss on Meagan's cheek, she was off.

Feeling restless and a little down, Meagan wondered what she should do with the rest of the day. The ball wasn't due to start until 7:30 so she had oodles of time.

She caught a glimpse of herself in the mirror in the sitting room. Jessie was right—she did look peaky. She was pale and there were dark rings under her eyes. Hardly surprising as she hadn't been sleeping well. Another wave of nausea washed over her. Goodness, she thought, I haven't felt like this since… And then her heart dropped to her shoes. No, it couldn't be! It wasn't possible, not with her medical history, she thought frantically. She was late now she took time to think about it. Only a few days, but late nevertheless. And she was as regular as clockwork. She sat down on the sofa. Was it possible? Could she be pregnant? She felt a flutter of excitement. No, don't think like that, she told herself firmly. This isn't a good thing. No matter how much you want a baby, you don't want to be a single mother. But if—despite all the odds against it—she was pregnant, what would she do? She squeezed her eyes shut. Unbidden, an image of her holding a tiny baby with Cameron looking at them both fondly filled her mind. Cameron! What would he think? But should she even tell him? What would be the point of that when he was leaving? But she was getting way ahead of herself. First she would need to find out one way or another if she was pregnant. Her heart plummeted at the thought. Even if she was, it might be another ectopic.

She could hardly bear the contrasting emotions of hope and terror. At the very least she needed to know whether she had conceived. Making up her mind, she grabbed her car keys from the bowl beside the door and jumped into her car. Very soon, one way or another, she would know.

Cameron, dressed in his dinner jacket, wrestled with his bow-tie. Ian stood watching him, his eyes round with excitement. He was wearing full Highland dress, with the exception of the *skean dubh*. He'd been mutinous when Cameron had refused to let him borrow his traditional knife.

'In a couple of years,' Cameron had promised his sulking son. Thankfully within minutes Ian had forgotten his disappointment and was hopping from one foot to another.

'Mummy wants you to help her fasten her necklace,' he said. Cameron was still sleeping in his own room in the west wing. Rachel had her own suite of rooms when she came to stay in the east of the house. He knew Rachel wanted him to move back in with her—too antediluvian to wait until we are married, darling, she had drawled—but he had resisted. Although he had agreed they should marry again, he wasn't ready yet for the kind of intimacy Rachel wanted. In fact, he wondered if he'd ever be ready. He closed his eyes against the image of Meagan in his arms. How could he take another woman to his bed when his mind was filled with the only woman who had ever really mattered to him?

'It's more appropriate, darling.' Rachel had tried to persuade him. 'After all, we'll soon be married.'

He frowned at the thought. Rachel was talking about going through the whole church ceremony

ANNE FRASER   239

again. Cameron dreaded the thought. It had been
bad enough the first time round. Why go to all
the bother of doing it all over again? But would
he mind if he was getting married for the right
reasons? If he was marrying Meagan, he would
want to shout it from the rooftops. Now, where
had that come from? He had promised himself
he wouldn't even think of Meagan, let alone
imagine getting married to her. Anyone would
think he was in love with her. His hands stopped
their restless and futile fiddling with his bow-tie.
In love with Meagan? He shook his head, trying
to clear it of the images of her—lying in his
arms, eyes soft and wondering after their love-
making, eyes sparkling as she splashed him with
water, and the last, most painful image of them
all, her eyes trying but failing to hide her hurt
and bewilderment when he had told her he was
going to remarry Rachel.

He cursed under his breath. Why couldn't he
have met Meagan just a few months before he
had? He would never have married Rachel had
she not been pregnant. But, then, and he glanced
down at his son who was practising his dancing,
there would have been no Ian. It wasn't worth

thinking about. None of it was worth thinking about. He was doing what he thought was right, and he needed to accept the hand life had dealt him, as he always had, and move on.

'I got tired waiting for you,' Rachel said, coming into the room. She looked breathtaking in a long silk sheath of deep blue that set off her eyes. She had twisted her hair into a sophisticated arrangement at the top of her head and finished her ensemble off with the pair of diamond earrings he had bought her on their wedding day. In her hand she held the matching necklace he had given her for their first wedding anniversary. 'Could you help me clasp this?'

She turned her back to him, offering him her long neck, and he quickly fastened the necklace.

'Ian,' she said to her son, 'do you want to check how your Uncle Simon is getting on?'

Ian ran out of the room, eager to help, as Rachel turned in Cameron's arms. She let her eyes linger on his.

'You look devastatingly handsome as always,' she said. 'There will hardly be a woman here tonight who won't envy me.' She traced a long finger between his brows.

'Why the frown, darling?'

Cameron took her hand and firmly placed it back by her side.

'Don't play games, Rachel,' he said, his voice deep with warning. 'You and I know exactly why we are getting married. There is no need to pretend love comes into it.'

'But love did come into it once,' she said quietly, 'and if only you'll let it, it could again.'

'I can't lie to you,' Cameron said. 'God knows, I never have and I am not going to start now. I will never change the way I feel about you. We are getting married and I will do my best to be a good husband to you, but that is all. You know I only agreed to this because of Ian.'

'Doesn't being a good husband mean you'll be sharing my bed?' Her eyes glittered up at him. 'That at least will make it…fun.'

Suddenly Cameron couldn't bear it any longer. He held Rachel away from him at arm's length. 'It's no use, is it?' he said sadly. 'If we get married again, it will be the worst mistake either of us will ever make. You don't love me and I—'

'Love someone else,' Rachel finished for him. 'Who is it?'

Cameron shook his head. 'It's really none of your business.'

'Oh, but it is,' Rachel spat. 'If you remember, I told you I would take custody of Ian if you ever married again, and I meant it. If I can't have you, be in no doubt that no one else will have you either.'

'Why do you care?' Cameron said wearily. 'You aren't going to pretend you love me. We both know it's not true. So why are you doing this? Why take Ian away from me? You know I can look after him better than you can.'

Rachel looked at him, her eyes moist. 'But that's just it,' she said. 'You have it all. But I, apart from my modelling, I have nothing. No one to love *me*.'

For a moment Cameron found his heart softening and he touched her cheek gently. But then he saw the flash of triumph in her eyes and knew that she had almost fooled him. There was really no doubt in his mind—the only reason Rachel wanted him was because she knew she couldn't have him and because she wanted to be Lady Rachel again. In her short, spoiled life her over-indulgent widower father had given her everything she had ever asked for, except the one thing she craved—someone of her own to love.

'Please, don't take my son away from me,' he said, his voice gruff with emotion. 'I'll beg you if I have to.'

Rachel looked at him coolly. For a moment Cameron saw something shift in her eyes. Was it sympathy? Regret? But, then just as quickly, her expression hardened.

'The choice is yours, Cameron. We get married and you both come with me—or we don't and I take Ian with me. You have to the end of the evening to let me know one way or another what your decision is.' And with a flash of violet eyes she left him standing alone.

CHAPTER EIGHT

MEAGAN finished drying herself after her bath. She stood in front of the mirror and surveyed the surprised—no, shocked—woman in front of her. She could hardly believe it. She dared hardly believe it. She was pregnant.

She finished drying her hair and started to get dressed, pulling her new dress over her head and letting it fall about her feet. She could feel the smooth silk cling to her body. It was far too early for her pregnancy to show and the dress emphasised her curves in the most flattering way. So this was what an expensive designer dress did for you, she thought. At least she wouldn't feel at a disadvantage next to Rachel tonight.

She still wasn't sure whether she should go to the ball. The thought of facing Cameron and Rachel made her stomach tighten with nervous tension. How would she feel seeing them together? And should she tell Cameron about the pregnancy? But even as she finished putting the finishing touches to her outfit, she knew she had no intention of telling him. It was too early in her pregnancy to be sure it would continue, and anyway what was the point? He and Rachel were getting married. Telling him about her own pregnancy would only—what? What would he do? Would he insist on staying with her? And if he did, would it be for all the wrong reasons? She also wanted her child to have two loving parents, but not at any cost. She couldn't bear it if Cameron stayed with her because of the baby. Unlike Rachel, she didn't want to be with someone who didn't love her.

She had never imagined that she would be a single mother, but life didn't always work out the way you planned, and this baby would be loved. Somehow she would make sure that he or she never wanted for anything.

She knew she had to go to the ball. She couldn't hide from Cameron, no matter how much she wanted to. She brushed her hair until it shone, letting it fall in a sheet around her shoulders. She finished her make-up, adding a final slick of lipstick. She was ready. Ready to face anything the evening could throw at her.

Just then there was a knock on the door and Jessie entered. 'Your carriage awaits,' she said.

'Oh, hello, Jessie. You look gorgeous,' Meagan greeted her. And she did. She had pulled her curls into an arrangement on the top of her head, leaving one or two tendrils to fall on either side of her face. She was wearing a full-length dress of cream with a tartan shawl around her shoulders. Gone was the slightly harassed-looking mother and in its place was a sophisticated and beautiful woman with sparkling eyes. Excitement had made her cheeks pink.

'You look pretty stunning yourself, Dr Galbraith. That dress is a perfect fit.'

'Thanks. And thanks for picking it out for me. But, Jessie, you needn't have taken the time to come and collect me. As I said before, I was— am—quite happy to drive myself. I would walk but in these heels I'm likely to break an ankle.'

'And I told you, I thought we could have a quiet drink here, just the two of us, before throwing ourselves into the mêlée. You've no idea how much I need a few minutes to myself right now. I seem to have been on my feet constantly since Simon and his guests arrived,' Jessie replied, settling herself into a chair.

'If you're sure? A white wine, then?'

Meagan poured a glass for Jessie and a soft drink for herself. She wouldn't be taking any chances. Not even the smallest glass until she was sure.

Jessie raised an eyebrow at Meagan's glass.

'Not having some wine yourself?'

'No,' Meagan replied. 'I'm not really much of a drinker.'

The two women sipped their drinks in companionable silence, each preoccupied with her own thoughts.

'Do you think we have to go?' Jessie said at last. 'In many ways I think I'd rather spend the evening here, just relaxing in the peace and quiet.'

'Mmm, tempting, isn't it? But I suspect our absence would be commented on.'

'You're right, I guess,' Jessie said, easing herself out of her chair. 'C'mon, then. Once more into the fray, dear friend. But first could I use your bathroom?'

'Of course,' Meagan said. 'I'll just get my bag from the bedroom.'

When Meagan returned it was to find Jessie standing looking distinctly curious. In her hand she held the discarded pregnancy test. In the end Meagan had decided to take the test from the surgery and do it in the privacy of her own home. She had been so rattled when she'd seen the result, It hadn't occurred to her to get rid of the evidence.

'Is this yours?' Jessie asked, holding out the test. 'I'm sorry, I know its really none of my business but when I saw it lying there I couldn't resist having a peep at the result.' Meagan blew out her cheeks. 'Positive!'

For a moment Meagan was tempted to deny that it was hers. She supposed she could say it belonged to a patient, but she knew Jessie was unlikely to believe her. Furthermore, she wanted to tell someone, and Jessie was really the only person she could tell.

'Yes. It's mine. And, yes, it is positive.'

'But I thought…'

'That I couldn't get pregnant? So did I. But it seems I was wrong,' Meagan finished for her. 'It seems my Fallopian tube wasn't as badly damaged as I'd thought.'

'But that's wonderful! Isn't it?' Jessie said.

'It's too early to say. There is a small chance it could be another ectopic, in which case, no, it wouldn't be good news.'

'When will you know? Who is the father? Is it Cameron's? Have you told him? What does he say about it? Is he pleased?' Meagan had to laugh at her friend's excitement.

'Hey, hey, slow down. I am not thinking about this until I know for certain that the pregnancy is viable. And then—and only then—will I decide if I should tell him.'

'It is Cameron's, then, isn't it?' Suddenly the excitement went out of Jessie's face. 'Oh, Meagan. And he's going to marry Rachel. You need to tell him before they announce their engagement. Surely this puts a whole different complexion on everything?'

'Why?' Meagan asked. She bit her lip. 'Don't you see? I can't tell him. What is he going to do? Choose between his son and a child who hasn't been born yet? It would be impossible.' She held up a hand to stop the words of protest. 'And say he did choose me. How would I ever know it was for the right reasons? If someone decides they want to be with me, it has to be because they love

me. I made do with second best before and I'll
never do that again.' To her chagrin she felt her
voice shake. But she had to make Jessie understand. 'And say the pregnancy didn't continue?
How could I bear knowing that he had given up
his son for nothing?' She shook her head sadly.
'No, Jessie. Please, understand. I have to do this
my way. By myself.'

'I still think he has the right to know,' Jessie
said stubbornly.

'But it's not up to you,' Meagan said, smiling
ruefully. 'Is it? Now, don't you think we'd
better go?'

By the time they arrived at the house, the ball
was in full swing. Meagan recognised several
faces that she had seen at the surgery as well as
those of the staff. Most of the men were dressed
in kilts while the women wore evening dress,
some like Jessie, with a tartan shawl matching
that of their partner's kilts around their shoulders.

The house was filled with the sound of accor-
dions and fiddles and many couples had already
taken to the floor and were dancing of Scottish

country dances. Meagan felt her feet tapping in rhythm. It had been so long since she had danced and she couldn't wait to take to the floor. Through the throng of guests she could make out the top of Cameron's head above those of the guests. Rachel, dressed in a rich blue gown with diamanté, clung to his arm possessively. They certainly made a striking couple, Meagan thought. Both so tall and handsome.

Cameron's head was bent as he listened attentively to what someone was saying. As the crowd parted, Meagan could see that it was Colin and Peggy. Back from their trip and looking rested and relaxed. She would have preferred to avoid Cameron for as long as possible, but she also knew she had to welcome Colin and his wife home.

As she approached the group she caught Cameron's eye. His gaze locked on hers and for a moment the world disappeared. She felt her heart pound and her knees grow weak. Here in front of her was everything she had ever wanted, but he belonged to someone else. Cameron bent down and kissed her cheek. 'You look stunning, Dr Galbraith,' he whispered in her ear.

Meagan felt herself grow warm. She felt her blush deepen as she caught Rachel's appraising look. She too bent and kissed her cheek before saying, 'Welcome, Meagan. The dress suits you. Your colour, I think.'

'Meagan!' Colin's voice drowned out her confusion. 'How are you? You look lovely, my dear.' He enveloped her in a hug.

'Yes, Meagan,' Peggy added. 'Quite beautiful. Although—' she peered short sightedly at Meagan '—you do look a little peaky. I hope you haven't been letting this man—' she nodded in Cameron's direction '—work you too hard.'

'I gather it's been pretty exciting here since I left,' Colin boomed. 'Rescues at sea and suchlike. Cameron has been telling me you coped like a pro.'

'Peggy, Colin.' Meagan kissed them both. 'It's wonderful to have you back. Did you have a good time?'

'Terrific.' Colin said. 'But we'll have you over for dinner so we can tell you all about it. How about tomorrow evening? You too, Cameron. You can both bring me up to speed with what has been happening at the same time.'

Just then an excited Ian and Effie came running over. Ian barrelled into his father's arms.

'Hey, slow down.' Cameron laughed, hugging his child. 'You almost knocked Dr Galbraith off her feet.'

Meagan caught her breath as she took in the scene they made. Cameron with his wife-to-be and son by his side. They were a family. Then Ian caught sight of Meagan and hurled himself at her.

'Where have you been? Why haven't you come to see me? When can we go sailing again?'

'It looks as if Ian is making remarkable progress,' Meagan said, laughing. 'Looking at him, you'd never guess he's just recovered from surgery.'

'I never did thank you for operating on our son. Cameron tells me it could have become serious if you hadn't been there,' Rachel said. She pulled her son towards her. 'I couldn't have borne it if anything had happened to him,' she continued softly. Meagan was surprised at the depth of emotion in Rachel's voice. And from the way she looked at her son, it seemed as if she meant every word she was saying. Of course she loved her child. What mother wouldn't? Perhaps she was only fighting for Cameron for her son's sake. Maybe she hadn't given her enough credit.

Nevertheless, Meagan didn't want to be around when they announced their engagement. It was bad enough having to stand here making polite conversation, without having to add her congratulations. She glanced down at Rachel's left hand. She wasn't wearing an engagement ring yet. So the announcement was still to come.

Meagan crouched in front of Ian. 'Hello, young man. Your daddy is right. You need to take it easy for a week or two until the wound in your tummy is completely healed. OK?'

'I will.' Ian promised. 'But I had to stay in bed for so many days and it was *so* boring. Daddy said I could come tonight for a little while. He said something good was going to happen and I should be there. But he wouldn't tell me what it was. Do you know, Dr Galbraith?'

Meagan closed her eyes briefly lest the child see the anguish she felt. When she opened them he was looking at her curiously. 'Are you all right? You looked a bit funny for a minute.' He pulled on his mother's hand. 'I think Dr Galbraith is sad about something, Mummy. Do you know what it is?'

As Meagan straightened she could feel Rachel's eyes on her. When she looked up, she found violet eyes staring into hers. Rachel was frowning. She looked from Meagan to Cameron and then back again.

'I suppose there are things that Dr Galbraith likes to keep to herself Ian,' she said.

'If you'll excuse me,' Meagan murmured through numb lips, 'I'll just go and find Jessie. Colin, Peggy, it's lovely to see you back. I'll look forward to seeing you tomorrow evening and hearing all about it.' Conscious being the focus of four pairs of puzzled eyes, Meagan turned and let the crowd swallow her.

She found Jessie surveying the buffet tables critically. The tables were loaded with every kind of food Meagan could imagine. From bowls of shellfish and platters of cold meats and salads to tiny cakes intricately decorated with swirls of chocolate and cream.

'Do you think there will be enough?' Jessie asked anxiously.

Meagan laughed. 'You have got to be kidding. There's enough there to feed the whole population of the island twice over. By the way, it looks like most of the island is here.'

Jessie glanced around the room. 'You should see the ball we have at New Year. It's even more packed. People come back to the island who have been away for years just for the ball. It's some night. Oh!' she added. 'I do hope you will be here then, Meagan.'

Meagan looked at her feet. She wouldn't be here. Now she was pregnant, there was no way she could stay. It would be impossible. Eventually everyone would find out that it was Cameron's child she was carrying. News would get back to him wherever he was. No, it was impossible. She could see that now. She felt a wave of sadness wash over her. Just when she had found somewhere she felt she belonged, she would have to up sticks and try and make a new life for herself and her child somewhere else. Jessie must have noticed how she was feeling. She touched her shoulder.

'Everything will work out, you'll see,' she said softly.

Before Meagan had a chance to reply, a tall, slim man with blond hair appeared at the table.

'Ah, Jessie,' he said. Although his accent was cultivated, his voice had the gentle island burr. 'I've been looking for you everywhere. Then it hit me. You'd be over worrying about the catering. Can't you take one night off at least, woman?'

Jessie blushed. Even before she introduced them, Meagan had a good idea who the young man was. Not least because of his striking resemblance to Cameron.

'Simon, can I introduce Dr Galbraith— Meagan? Meagan— Simon Stuart.'

'Nice to meet you, Meagan,' he said, grinning at Meagan, before turning back to Jessie just as the band was striking up another tune. 'May I have the pleasure of both you ladies for the next dance? The Dashing White Sergeant, I believe, so I need both of you.'

Now that I'm here, Meagan thought, I may as well enjoy myself. Moments later she was being whirled around the dance floor. Out of the corner of her eye she could see Cameron's eyes on her, but he was too far away for her to read his expression.

The set came to an end just in front of Cameron. Before she could catch her breath, he was leading her back onto the dance floor for a waltz. She let herself relax into his arms as he moved with effortless grace around the floor. She, on the other hand, had never been much of a dancer and was soon finding herself treading on Cameron's toes.

'Just relax,' he said, 'and follow me. Don't think too much about your feet.' He was right. As soon as she stopped thinking about the steps, they were dancing as if they had always partnered one another.

Meagan closed her eyes, breathing in the faint scent of aftershave. She could feel the pressure of his hand on the small of her back. This could be the last time he ever held her, she thought miserably.

'You look lost in thought.' Cameron bent his head and whispered in her ear. 'Penny for them?'

The heat was making Meagan's head spin.

'I was just wondering when you're going to announce your engagement.'

She felt rather than heard his intake of breath.

'My engagement,' he said slowly. He glanced

around before manoeuvring Meagan towards an open door.

'Let's gets some air,' he said.

Out on the verandah it was cool. Winter wasn't far away, Meagan thought. What would it be like here in the winter? And where would she be?

She shivered. Wherever she was, she would be alone. But, please, God, if her pregnancy was to continue, she would have her child—their child.

Cameron slipped off his jacket and wrapped it around her shoulders. She could feel the heat of him in its warmth.

'What are you going to do?' he asked.

For a moment she thought he was referring to the baby. But then realised he couldn't be. There was no way he could know.

'About what?' she asked, more sharply than she had intended.

'About the permanent position here,' he said. 'I've no doubt Colin will want you to stay on. In fact, he's hinted that he wants to offer you the position tomorrow at dinner. I've told him I think you'd be an excellent choice. And you would be, Meagan,' he added softly. 'Any practice would be lucky to get you.'

'Does he know you are leaving?' Meagan asked.

'No. Only you and Jessie know so far. I haven't had a chance to tell him.'

'It puts me in a difficult position, then, doesn't it? He couldn't cope here alone if we both left. And as you pointed out before, it's not that easy to find someone who will want to live here. Who will really love this place and want to make a difference here.'

Cameron pulled a hand through his hair. Meagan had to fight to resist the temptation to smooth it away from his eyes. He looked... almost broken, she thought. She hadn't seen him look like that before. Vulnerable, not in control.

'I wish there was another way,' he said. He touched her hair and in the light of the moon Meagan could see the pain in his eyes. 'I wish...' He left the sentence unfinished.

'You wish what?' she said, her heart pounding.

Cameron let his hand follow the planes of her face. He tipped her chin and looked straight into her eyes.

'I wish I had met you first,' he said hoarsely. He lowered his head and covered her mouth with his. Meagan froze, but then almost as if her body was separate to her will, she felt it melt into his. Just once more, she thought, then I can leave him.

They kissed hungrily, oblivious to the fact that there was someone in the shadows behind them watching. Eventually they broke apart, both breathing heavily. 'My God, Meagan,' Cameron said. 'I want you so much.'

'But you can't have me. And I can't have you.' Meagan said wearily. 'We both know that.'

Cameron pulled her back into his arms. She rested there for a moment, her head against his chest. She could hear the rhythmic pounding of his heart.

'There has to be a way,' he said grimly. 'I have to find a way.'

Rachel watched as the two figures clung to each other. She had suspected that Meagan was in love with Cameron, but until now had had no idea that he felt the same way. When she had asked him if there was anyone else, it had been a stab in the dark, but the way he had looked at Meagan, the way he kissed her, she knew instinctively that he loved Meagan in a way that he had never loved her. She stepped forward as the two drew apart.

'Is there something you want to tell me, Cameron?' she said quietly.

CHAPTER NINE

MEAGAN was horrified. How long had Rachel been watching from the shadows? What had she seen and heard?

'Rachel,' Cameron said heavily. 'You are right. We do need to talk.'

Meagan was deeply embarrassed. 'I'm sorry, Rachel,' she blurted. 'I should go. Leave you two alone.' And before anyone could stop her she slipped back inside.

She found her bag and coat where she had left them. She thought about saying goodnight to Jessie but, seeing her dancing with Simon, her face lifted to his and her eyes glowing with pleasure, she decided against it. Besides, she couldn't face Jessie right now.

Unseen, she went back outside. The darkness was complete. For a moment the moon peeped out from behind clouds, illuminating the road home, but Meagan was barely aware of it. All she wanted to do was get away as quickly as possible from Grimsay House, from Cameron and from Rachel. Despite the cool night air, her cheeks still burned with shame. How could she have let Cameron kiss her and—worse—kiss him back? It didn't matter what their feelings for one another were—he was committed to Rachel and Ian, and she had no right to come between them. Meagan groaned. Hadn't she vowed that she would never be the 'other woman' after what Charlie and his mistress had done to her?

As the moon dipped behind the clouds, Meagan wished she had thought to ask to borrow a torch, but it was too late now. There was no way she was going back inside. All she wanted to do right now was get to the safety of her cottage, undress and go to bed.

As she half ran down the road, her shoe caught in the hem of her dress. Stopping to remove her high heels, she took a couple of deep steadying breaths. She *had* to calm down. She had allowed Cameron to kiss her, but it had been a good bye. Hopefully he'd be able to persuade Rachel that their affair was over—had never really started.

Cameron could never be hers. She would have to accept that, no matter how painful, and move on with her life. She couldn't stay here. She knew that with heart-breaking certainty.

She stubbed her bare toe on a loose stone and yelped. Damn, damn, damn, she cursed. Why does life have to be so bloody difficult? She let the tears that had been clogging her throat for the last half-hour fall. There was no one to see and she deserved a good cry.

She was halfway home when the moon disappeared completely. Away from the lights of Grimsay House she was plunged into total darkness, unable to see the hand in front of her face, let alone the road. For a moment she considered retracing her steps and returning to the ball, but only for a second. She knew deep down inside that she wasn't up to a scene. No doubt she'd have to face Rachel some time, but not tonight. It was more than she could bear.

Suddenly she felt the hard surface of the road give way. Surprised, she stumbled and lost her footing. She went down heavily, twisting her ankle in the process. For a few minutes she sat, rubbing her ankle, waiting for the shock and nausea to pass. The pain was excruciating. Had she broken it? she wondered. She waited a few moments longer, hoping the pain would subside. Once she had caught her breath and the pain had faded slightly, she attempted to stand, tentatively testing her weight on the foot. It was no use. She couldn't walk. Mentally she calculated the distance to her house. She had been over halfway when she had fallen. Her cottage was just a few hundred yards in front of her—or was it behind her? Without any light to guide her, she was disoriented. She should be able to see the lights of Grimsay House and get her bearings that way. But she had been going downhill and around a corner. The lights had been hidden from her view by the hill. That was one of the reasons she had lost her footing.

Don't panic, she thought. Eventually someone would drive down the road and with a bit of luck she'd be able to attract their attention. And if not, well, she had her mobile in her bag.

She felt in her handbag for her phone and when her fingers located the slim, hard shape, she felt relieved. That was until she realised there was no signal. She felt tears of frustration prick her eyes.

Then she remembered. Hadn't some one once told her that you could send a text sometimes even if you couldn't get a signal? It was worth a go anyway. Quickly she tapped in a message to Jessie and pressed the 'send' button. Just as quickly a message came back telling her that her message had failed.

Meagan took a deep breath. She couldn't stay there all night. Especially as a couple of cars whizzed past her, unable to hear her cries for help. She would just have to hop or crawl towards her cottage.

But a short while later Meagan knew she was lost. She had no idea whether she was getting closer to help or further away. She couldn't even find the road to follow it. She decided to rest for a while before trying again.

As she sat shivering on the damp, peaty ground, her thoughts turned to the tiny life growing inside her.

Mentally calculating dates in her head, she worked out the earliest time she could have a scan. She would be around four weeks, she thought. She would need to be a bit further on before she could have a scan that would tell her for certain if the baby was growing in her womb or in her Fallopian tube.

Poor tiny baby, she thought. You really do have the odds stacked against you. But perhaps this child would be a fighter. Like its parents. The thought spurred her on. She couldn't stay here all night and she needed to keep moving. It was a cold night and if she stayed where she was she would become hypothermic. She needed to keep moving. She struggled to her feet, but only managed to hop a few steps before having to rest again. There was nothing for it. She would have to crawl. She ripped a strip off the bottom of her dress with her teeth and used the fabric to bind her ankle as best she could. She smiled inwardly. She was a bit like Cinderella—going to the ball, only for her finery to be turned back to rags. And as for the prince, well. Still, a dress could be replaced. But what about Rachel and Cameron? Could their fractured relationship ever be mended—even for Ian's sake? Her thoughts turned to Cameron. Had he managed to persuade Rachel that what she had seen meant nothing? Would they be announcing their engagement right now?

In the perfect stillness of the night she could hear the waves lapping against the shore. Did that mean she was moving in the right direction? She carried on crawling.

How she loved it here. It would have been the perfect place to bring up a child. For a moment she left herself imagine how it might have been. Her child growing up free to run wild. To learn what it was like to live in a community where everyone helped each other. Where you knew and cared about your neighbour. Where life and death was part of the everyday fabric.

The thought of death made her shiver. What if she couldn't find her way to help? What if she ended up there all night?

She shook her head to banish the thought. That simply wasn't going to happen. Not while she had a breath in her body. She carried on, making her painful way inch by inch in the direction of the sound of the sea. But despite her efforts she seemed to be making no progress. It was possible even that she was moving further away.

Just when she thought she couldn't force herself to go any further, she heard a faint sound in the wind. She stopped and listened attentively. She was so cold. So cold and so tired.

The sound came again. She hadn't been mistaken. Someone was calling her name. She made herself get to her feet. In the near distance she could make out a familiar broad frame. It was Cameron! He was carrying a torch and sweeping the area from side to side. She called out and waved. And then finally he was coming for her. Running and calling her name. As he reached her, she felt her last bit of strength give way as she was lifted in strong, comforting arms.

'My, God Meagan, are you all right?' he was asking, and she could hear the fear in his voice.

'My ankle,' she managed. 'I think it's broken. I couldn't find my way home. I was lost and I was scared.' She felt her voice break as the fear she had been holding back threatened to overwhelm her.

'You're not lost any more, my darling,' he said. 'I've found you and I'm never going to let you go again.'

Meagan was barely aware of Cameron carrying her back to her cottage. She felt herself being lowered onto the sofa before being covered with a thick blanket. Then he took hands and was rubbing them vigorously between his.

'Lie there for a moment while I rekindle the fire,' he ordered.

'Stop bossing me about,' she mumbled grumpily, burrowing deep into the blanket. She couldn't stop shivering.

As soon as he had the fire blazing, he returned to her side. She felt a sting in her thigh.

'Ouch.' She glared at him.

'Just some analgesia,' he said. His hands dipped under the blanket and before Meagan knew what was happening he was removing her sodden dress.

'Do you mind?' she said, trying to force his hands away.

He grinned at her feeble efforts, before slipping in beside her and pulling her naked body close, carefully avoiding her injured foot. Almost instantly she could feel the heat of his body begin to suffuse hers.

'Just relax,' he said. 'Once we've got you warm I'll have a look at that ankle.'

Meagan felt a welcoming lethargy steal over

her body. Although there was so much she wanted to ask him, she couldn't stop her eyes from closing. At last she gave in to sleep.

When she next opened her eyes, she was still held firmly in Cameron's arms and light was beginning to trickle through the curtains. She lifted her eyes slightly and found his.

'You're awake, then?' he whispered. 'How does the ankle feel?'

Meagan tried to move it, but it was tightly bound. Cameron must have bandaged it while she'd slept. Although it throbbed, she thought with relief that it probably wasn't broken after all.

'It's a little bit sore,' she said, 'but nothing a couple of strong painkillers couldn't sort out. Do you think it's broken?'

'I can't be sure until we have it X rayed, but I think you've got away with a bad sprain. Mind you, as you know, they can be almost as painful as a break.'

'How did you find me?' she asked.

He held her closer, resting his chin on top of her head.

'With great difficulty. God, you scared me, Meagan.'

'Does your fiancée know you're here? she said suddenly. She lifted her face so she could see his eyes

'She's not my fiancée.' he said, and he grinned. Meagan caught her breath. He looked just like he had that first night. Like a mischievous schoolboy. Or a fallen angel.

'She's called it off. She says she's still going and I can keep Ian here with me.'

'She what?' Meagan said, her heart beginning to race. 'Why?'

'She said she suddenly realised that I truly didn't love her. That I never could. She said she could see I loved you, and what sort of woman did I take her for if she thought she could marry a man who was in love with someone else?' He pulled Meagan close. She could feel his lips on her hair. Her heart was beating wildly. She felt a rush of happiness that made her stomach flip.

'And are you? In love with someone else?'

'Don't you know?' Then he was kissing her and she was drowning. The blanket fell away as his hands searched frantically for her bare skin. He pulled her closer and she was left in no doubt of his desire for her. But he still hadn't answered her question. Oh, she knew he wanted her. But that wasn't the same as being in love with her. She had to know. Reluctantly she pulled away.

'What is it you want from me, Cameron?' she asked, her eyes searching his.

He stopped talking. Then he took a deep breath.

'When Rachel and I finished talking I knew I had to tell you. I came down here straight away, but you weren't here. I knew something must have happened. I was scared out of my wits. Especially...' He broke off.

'Especially...?' Meagan prompted.

'Especially when I knew how cold the night would get. And how dark. I knew something must have happened to you. My God, if I hadn't come, you could still be out there.'

'But you did find me,' she soothed. 'But what now?'

'Don't you see, Meagan? This means we can be together. I can stay with Ian and we can be together. You, me, Ian and the baby.'

Suddenly Meagan felt her blood run cold. She pushed him away.

'What do you mean?'

'Jessie told me,' Cameron said, seemingly oblivious to Meagan's reaction. 'I know you made her promise not to, but she thought I should know. She hadn't realised that Rachel and I had already agreed to part. And she was scared that I was about to make a mistake that would haunt me for the rest of my life. She was only thinking of our happiness.'

'Well, she had no right,' Meagan said through stiff lips. 'It was up to me to tell you. If I ever did.' Her heart felt leaden. Would he have come to her if he hadn't known she was pregnant?

'Of course I needed to know,' Cameron retorted. 'Oh, Meagan, I can't believe you were going to keep it from me.'

'And did she tell you there's a chance that this pregnancy will not continue?'

Cameron lifted the blanket and stood. He was still dressed in his dinner shirt and trousers, although with his stubble he looked different from the immaculately dressed man of the night before. Somehow Meagan preferred him like this. He looked at her, puzzled.

'You mean because of your previous history? I admit I hadn't thought about that. My poor love. You must be worried. But there is no reason that this pregnancy won't be normal. We can scan you up at the hospital, then we'll know for sure.'

'Is that why you came here? A second woman pregnant with your child? Are you determined to do the right thing by me, too?'

'What do you mean?' Cameron narrowed his eyes at her. 'If you are suggesting that I want to marry you simply because you are carrying my child, you are mad. I did that once—and look at the consequences. I'm hardly likely to make the same mistake twice.'

'What if I don't want to marry you?' she said.

For a moment Cameron looked floored. He frowned.

'Don't you want to get married?' he said. 'I thought…'

'Thought what exactly? That I would be so relieved that you wanted to be my protector and the father of my child that I would be flattered, even grateful for your proposal? It's a whole new world now, Cameron. Two people don't have to get married just because they have conceived a child together. And what if I lose this baby? How will you feel then? Trapped?' She laughed, but it was a strangled sound that held no joy.

'I could never feel trapped married to you,' Cameron protested. 'And if by some awful chance we lose this baby, we'll try for another.'

'But this could be my last chance. If I they take out the other Fallopian tube, I'll never be able to conceive naturally.' She shook her head. It was no use. It had all happened so fast. Meeting Cameron again, finding that her feelings for him had never truly gone away, fighting it and then finally giving in and accepting that there would never be any one else for her, despite the fact that he belonged to some one else. Then the pregnancy and mixed emotions of joy and fear that had come with the knowledge. She was terrified, she admitted to herself. She had never been more scared in all her life. Not even out there on the moors. If she dared even think that this child growing inside her was a possibility, maybe she would jinx it.

She looked at Cameron. In the faint glow of the dying fire his eyes glinted as he waited for her to say something else.

'You were right back then that first day on the

hill,' she said finally, with a faint smile. 'Our timing has always been wrong. I don't know what to do any more. And when I don't know what to do, I find the best thing is to do nothing. At the very least let us wait. We will know about the baby one way or another soon enough.'

'But I have already told you, I want you regardless. I love you—I realise I have never loved anyone the way I love you. You are the only woman I imagine myself growing old with, the only person I can see by my side. With you life will never stop being an adventure. You know as well as I do that we were meant to be together. We have wasted enough years as it is.' Cameron grabbed her by the shoulders, her fingers biting into her. His eyes blazed with his need to make her believe him.

'And Ian? What about him?' Meagan asked. 'I can't imagine he'll be too happy to have a stepmother.'

'Ian will be happy as long as he knows that he is loved. I wouldn't be proposing to you if I didn't think you cared for him. You do, don't you?'

Meagan smiled, thinking of the little boy. 'I can't imagine anyone not caring for him.'

'Then it's settled? You'll marry me? As soon as possible?'

It would be so easy, Meagan thought, to give in to this man. She wanted nothing more than to spend the rest of her life with him. But could she take the risk? What if she lost this baby and they drifted apart—just like she and Charlie had? It would break her heart. And it wouldn't be fair on Ian. The child had known enough disruption as it was.

'I…I don't know. Cameron, you have to give me time. I can't…won't make any decisions. Not until I know about the baby.'

Cameron looked down at her, defeated.

'Get some sleep, Meagan. We'll talk again later. Right now you need to rest.'

When Meagan opened her eyes again the sun was shining weakly and Mrs MacLeod was making up the fire.

'You're awake, I'll just let Cameron know. He told me I had to phone him the minute you woke up. My, my,' she went on, 'I don't think I've seen him this agitated since he was sent away to school.'

Meagan had a sudden glimpse of a young boy

in short trousers being taken away to school. She could almost see the resolute line of the mouth and the young Cameron's determination not to show any fear.

'You have known him a long time, then?'

'All his life. I have been at the house ever since he and Simon were born. Speaking of which, the news is that Simon has just gone and proposed to Jessie. And she's accepted him.' Flora gave a satisfied nod of her head. 'And that's exactly as it should be. She says to tell you she'll be down soon, but Cameron has forbidden visitors until he says otherwise.'

Meagan sat up, taking the cup of tea Flora was passing to her.

She was delighted for Jessie. She guessed her friend would be down to tell her all about it soon.

'Speaking of which, I gather the wedding at the house is off. Not that I am surprised.' She gave Meagan a shrewd look. 'I've suspected for some time his affections lie in another direction altogether.'

For a moment, Meagan felt her heart lift. She raised an eyebrow in the housekeeper's direction. 'Oh?' She couldn't help herself. She had to know what Flora meant.

'Oh, don't you go pretending that you don't know that he's smitten with you. I had given you more credit than that. I don't think you're the kind of woman to play games with a man's heart.' She looked sharply at Meagan, making it clear that any woman who played around with her beloved Cameron's heart would be answering to her.

Meagan's own heart was beginning to beat faster. Could it be true? Could Cameron really want her—not because she was carrying his child or because he needed a surrogate mother for his son?

Just then the man in question opened the door and strode into the room. At the sight of him, Meagan's breath caught in her throat.

Mrs Macleod took one look at his expression and decided to beat a hasty retreat. 'I'll be down later with your supper, dear,' she said, before closing the door behind her. Cameron looked as if he hadn't slept all night.

After a quick examination of her foot and pronouncing himself satisfied with his earlier diagnosis, he glared down at Meagan. Seeing his expression—challenging, demanding but just a little bit scared—she knew the truth. He loved her!

'Just tell me,' he demanded without preamble. 'Tell me you feel the way I do. As long as I know that I can wait.' He pulled a hand through his hair in the gesture Meagan was coming to know so well. 'If you don't love me…well, I guess I'll have to live with that.'

'Of course I love you, you idiot,' Meagan capitulated. 'I guess I have loved you since the night we met.' She could read the triumph in his deep brown eyes. He grinned.

'Well, then, baby or no baby, you will have to marry me.' He held a finger to her lips. 'I am warning you, Meagan, I won't stop asking you until you say yes.'

Meagan sank back on her makeshift bed. 'Then, you great big stubborn man, I guess I will just have to say yes. It seems it's the only way I am going to get any peace.'

She had just enough time to see his smile before once again he was kissing her.

'My love, *mo ghràigh*, I'll love you until the end of time,' he whispered between kisses.

'Just you see that you do, Dr Stuart,' she said. And deep in her heart she knew that, whatever the future would bring, she could face anything with this man by her side.

MEDICAL™

──∿── *Large Print* ──∿──

Titles for the next six months...

August

CHILDREN'S DOCTOR, SOCIETY BRIDE	Joanna Neil
THE HEART SURGEON'S BABY SURPRISE	Meredith Webber
A WIFE FOR THE BABY DOCTOR	Josie Metcalfe
THE ROYAL DOCTOR'S BRIDE	Jessica Matthews
OUTBACK DOCTOR, ENGLISH BRIDE	Leah Martyn
SURGEON BOSS, SURPRISE DAD	Janice Lynn

September

THE CHILDREN'S DOCTOR'S SPECIAL PROPOSAL	Kate Hardy
ENGLISH DOCTOR, ITALIAN BRIDE	Carol Marinelli
THE DOCTOR'S BABY BOMBSHELL	Jennifer Taylor
EMERGENCY: SINGLE DAD, MOTHER NEEDED	Laura Iding
THE DOCTOR CLAIMS HIS BRIDE	Fiona Lowe
ASSIGNMENT: BABY	Lynne Marshall

October

A FAMILY FOR HIS TINY TWINS	Josie Metcalfe
ONE NIGHT WITH HER BOSS	Alison Roberts
TOP-NOTCH DOC, OUTBACK BRIDE	Melanie Milburne
A BABY FOR THE VILLAGE DOCTOR	Abigail Gordon
THE MIDWIFE AND THE SINGLE DAD	Gill Sanderson
THE PLAYBOY FIREFIGHTER'S PROPOSAL	Emily Forbes

◉™ MILLS & BOON®

0709 LP 2P P1 Medical

MEDICAL™

Large Print

November

THE SURGEON SHE'S BEEN WAITING FOR   Joanna Neil
THE BABY DOCTOR'S BRIDE   Jessica Matthews
THE MIDWIFE'S NEW-FOUND FAMILY   Fiona McArthur
THE EMERGENCY DOCTOR   Margaret McDonagh
CLAIMS HIS WIFE
THE SURGEON'S SPECIAL DELIVERY   Fiona Lowe
A MOTHER FOR HIS TWINS   Lucy Clark

December

THE GREEK BILLIONAIRE'S LOVE-CHILD   Sarah Morgan
GREEK DOCTOR, CINDERELLA BRIDE   Amy Andrews
THE REBEL SURGEON'S PROPOSAL   Margaret McDonagh
TEMPORARY DOCTOR, SURPRISE   Lynne Marshall
FATHER
DR VELASCOS' UNEXPECTED BABY   Dianne Drake
FALLING FOR HER MEDITERRANEAN   Anne Fraser
BOSS

January

THE VALTIERI MARRIAGE DEAL   Caroline Anderson
THE REBEL AND THE BABY DOCTOR   Joanna Neil
THE COUNTRY DOCTOR'S DAUGHTER   Gill Sanderson
SURGEON BOSS, BACHELOR DAD   Lucy Clark
THE GREEK DOCTOR'S PROPOSAL   Molly Evans
SINGLE FATHER: WIFE AND MOTHER   Sharon Archer
WANTED

MILLS & BOON®